A Demon's Plaything

The Elite Guards

Amelia Hutchins

A Demon's Plaything

Copyright ©February9th2019 Amelia Hutchins

This book is a work of fiction. Names, characters, places and incidents are either the product of the author's imagination or are used fictitiously. Any resemblance to actual persons, living or dead, or to actual events or locales is entirely coincidental.

This book in its entirety and in portions is the sole property of Amelia Hutchins.

A Demon's Plaything Copyright ©2019 by Amelia Hutchins. All rights reserved, including the right to reproduce this book, or portions thereof, in any form. No part of this text may be reproduced, transmitted, downloaded, decompiled, reverse engineered, or stored in or introduced into any information storage and retrieval system, in any form or by any means, whether electronic or mechanical without the express written permission of the author. The scanning, uploading and distribution of this book via the Internet or via any other means without the permission of the publisher is illegal and punishable by law. Please purchase only authorized electronic editions and do not participate in or encourage electronic piracy of copyrighted materials. This eBook is licensed for your personal enjoyment only. This eBook may not be re-sold or given away to other people. If you would like to share this book with another person, please purchase an additional copy for each recipient. If you're reading this book and did not purchase it, or it was not purchased for your use only, then please return to Amazon.com Kindle Direct and purchase your own copy.

Thank you for respecting the hard work of this author.

The unauthorized reproduction or distribution of this copyrighted work is illegal. Criminal copyright infringement, including infringement without monetary gain, is investigated by the FBI and is punishable by up to 5 years in federal prison and a fine of $250,000.

Authored By: Amelia Hutchins
Copy edited by: E & F Indie Services
Edited by: E & F Indie Services
Published in (United States of America)
10 9 8 7 6 5 4 3 2 1

Also by Amelia Hutchins

The Fae Chronicles
Fighting Destiny
Taunting Destiny
Escaping Destiny
Seducing Destiny
Unraveling Destiny
Embracing Destiny - *Coming Soon (Final Book)*

**The Elite Guards
(Part of the Fae Chronicles)**
A Demon's Dark Embrace
Claiming the Dragon King
A Demon's Plaything
A Winter Court

**A Guardian's Diary
Stands alone**
Darkest Before Dawn
Death before Dawn
Midnight Rising - *Coming Soon (Final Book)*

**Playing with Monsters series
(Part of the Fae Chronicles)**
Playing with Monsters
Sleeping with Monsters
Becoming his Monster
Last Monster Book *TBA*

UPCOMING SERIES

<u>Wicked Knights</u>
Oh, Holy Knight
If She's Wicked 2019

<u>A Crown of Ashes</u>
Coming Soon

If you're following the series for the Fae Chronicles, Elite Guards, and Monsters, reading order is as follows:

Fighting Destiny
Taunting Destiny
Escaping Destiny
Seducing Destiny
A Demon's Dark Embrace
Playing with Monsters
Unraveling Destiny
Sleeping with Monsters
Claiming the Dragon King
Oh, Holy Knight
Becoming his Monster
A Demon's Plaything
A Winter Court
If She's Wicked 2019 (Full story from Oh, Holy Knight)

WARNING!

STOP!! READ THE WARNING BELOW BEFORE PURCHASING THIS BOOK.

TRIGGER WARNING: This book contains scenes of graphic violence and does have adult language and sexually explicit scenes that may be offensive to some readers. The book does include the subject matter of rape. Rape isn't a joke, nor is it used for titillation in this book. If you know someone or have been a victim of rape yourself, get help. Don't let the asshole get away with it because chances are, your attacker will do it to someone else. You're not alone in this. Thousands of people are raped daily; there are hundreds of people who go free after attacking their victim because the victim is afraid to report or discuss the crime for a variety of reasons. No means no. If you or someone you know has been a victim of rape, get help. **RAINN** is available in many countries, and is a free confidential hotline. It is free to call and available 24/7 call **1-800-656-HOPE**.

Warning: This book is **dark**. It's **sexy**, hot, and **intense**. The author is human, you are as well. Is the book perfect? It's as perfect as I could make it. Are there mistakes? Probably, then again, even **New York Times top published** books have minimal mistakes because like me, they have **human editors**. There are words in this book that won't be found in the standard dictionary, because they were created to set the stage for a paranormal-urban fantasy world. Words such as 'sift', 'glamoured', and 'apparate' are common in paranormal books and give better description to the action in the

WARNING! (CONT'D)

story than can be found in standard dictionaries. They are intentional and not mistakes.

About the hero: chances are you may **not** fall instantly in **love** with him, that's because **I don't write men you instantly love**; you grow to love them. I don't believe in **instant-love**. I write flawed, raw, caveman-like **assholes** that eventually let you see their redeeming qualities. They are **aggressive, assholes**, one step above a caveman when we meet them. You may *not* even like him by the time you finish this book, but I promise you will **love** him by the end of this **series**.

About the heroine: There is a chance, that you might think she's a bit naïve or weak, but then again who starts out as a badass? Badasses are a product of growth and I am going to put her through **hell**, and you get to watch **her** come up **swinging** every time I knock her on her ass. That's just how I do things. How she reacts to the set of circumstances she is put through, may not be how you as the reader, or I as the author would react to that same situation. Everyone reacts differently to circumstances and how Ciara responds to her challenges, is how I see her as a character and as a person.

I don't write love stories: I write fast paced, knock you on your ass, make you sit on the edge of your seat wondering what happens in the next kind of books. If you're looking for cookie cutter romance, this isn't for you. If you can't handle the ride, ***un-buckle your seatbelt and get out of the roller-coaster car now***. **If not, you've been warned.** If nothing outlined above bothers you, carry on and **enjoy the ride!**

Dedication

This one is for you, the forgotten one.
To the ones who dance to their own drumbeat. You are your own kind of beautiful. Don't ever let them dim your sparkle to fit in. To the broken ones trying put their puzzle back together. Sometimes, being broken is beautiful, and that chaos makes you shine ever so brightly among the dull, perfectness of everyone else. Dust yourself off, stand proud, and show the world that sometimes, broken things shine brighter than anything else.

A Demon's PlaythinG

The Elite Guards

A Demon's Playthimg

The Elite Guards

Chapter One

Lilith watched the moon rising high into the ebony sky, her ice blue eyes following it until it bathed the Night Court in shadows, shadows she loved and preferred over people. The night was hers to rule, to devour the light of any who dared to enter her fortress. All but one man was brazen enough to cross her path, and he was the King and her father.

It was what had forced her to be here tonight, unwilling. Once a year he would summon her here, give her a list of her princess duties, and then she'd retire to her mother's castle, the Castle of Shadows. It was her sanctuary away from the court she hated and loathed. Plus, the growing list of princes from other castes or courts was a never-ending nightmare, one she wanted to avoid at all cost. Unlike her many sisters who wanted to marry for hierarchy and their place in it.

Lilith, though, she was the legal heir by court law. The highest prize that none had the balls to try for. She was her father's heir by right, his only legitimate child.

She was also the only one who didn't want the burden of the crown he wore, not that she'd made that notion well-known.

"The king is ready for you, Princess Lilith," Lothian muttered as his dark, heavy gaze gave her a withering once-over.

She swiped at an invisible piece of lint on her midnight colored dress and righted her quiver that was slung over her shoulder. "Any idea why I'm here earlier than normal?" she queried, her ice blue eyes slowly settling on his as she sucked her bottom lip between her teeth and waited for his answer.

"That is something only he can tell you, if you'll just follow me," he indicated with a wave of his arm towards the high, double doors that were glinted with moonstones. "He awaits you."

She frowned, her face tightening with concernment as she took the lead, dismissing the guard who had to be as old as the castle stones and yet didn't look a single day over thirty. A benefit of being immortal, un-aging beauty that gave them a certain flawlessness humans and other creatures prayed or sold their soul for.

Inside the braziers were lit, the room was bathed in light and beauty as the heady scent of the midnight blue citrus trees bloomed. Her footsteps were light over the moonstones that covered the floor in a delicate pattern of the Tree of Life, from which Faery drew its power. A giant picture of the Stag covered the wall behind the raised dais of her father's throne; his gentle matching eyes found her and softened as she approached.

"Lilith," he uttered thickly with sadness, as if she was a mere child instead of a full-grown woman. "Every year you look more like her."

Her mother. Liliana of the Shadow Court, who the Horde had slain for fun when her father had refused the tithe they'd demanded. Only where her mother's eyes had been as dark as the shadows, Lilith's were ice blue, a gift from her father's bloodline and the mark of the true heir to his court.

"I wouldn't know what she looked like, now would I?" she asked, her seething tone mocking him for his weakness to protect her mother against the Horde. Her father had taken down everything of her mother's, including the pictures that had once filled this palace. He allowed no memory of her to remain, not even her daughter.

"You have only to look into the mirror to find her," he admonished, hurt filling his words as he watched her slow approach. "I've called you here to inform you of your betrothal," he said after a moment.

"I have no plan to marry anyone," she countered icily, her heart thundering as his words registered in her mind.

"The tithe is due, Lilith. As it is, the Horde has been merciful enough to allow a marriage in its place, since once again, we cannot afford to pay it. I don't need to remind you what happens when you fail to pay the tithe to them, do I? You will marry a prince. A brother to the king, and become the first Night Court princess to raise our standards, to rise above being a lesser Fae, and birth a high born child into our court. It isn't a choice. You will do this."

"No, I will not," she hissed, her eyes burning with liquid blue flames. "They took from us, and now they demand we give more?" she scoffed. "And you, you bow to no one. You're the King of the Night Court, we don't need to raise our place in the courts, they all fear us, and they fear me. We have always ruled through that fear, and so we shall continue."

"They're offering the other courts a similar bargain, and when they accept it, they will also rise in power. You're the last remaining heir to the Court of Shadows, and my heir to the Night Court, Lilith. You will do this!"

"Marry him off to one of the others who will bow at his feet and worship him, not me. They murdered my mother! You cannot ask me to do this!"

"You will do this because I am the king and your father. You will do this, or you will be removed to allow the heir brands to pass to my next child. I cannot allow what happened before to happen again."

"The only way to do that is to kill me," she chuckled and then paused as she took in the warriors who waited for her next move, hands ready on their weapons as they watched her. "Which you'd do because power means everything to you, doesn't it?"

"I will not cower before the other courts, Lilith. I have not been kind to them, as I have held both titles until a time you came to power, and still, I held your title so that you could hide away to mourn a mother you never knew. The Horde took from everyone, everyone! They took my mate, the love of my life from this very room, and slaughtered her before my eyes. I have known pain at their hands, and yet even I can forgive. The new king's rule is blessed by the Goddess herself. You carry the blood of Artemis in your veins, and the blood of the darkest courts. You will do this for this court, and after you've secured a child, you can decide your own fate, daughter. Life is made by those who know when to bow, and when to strike. Now is the time to bow. The lands are dying and we with them. They wage war against those who trespass against this world, and I gave my word that I would do what was needed to help them. You don't have to like this, but you will do this or else so help me, girl. After a time, you will be free to leave him and the child. If you choose to retire to your mother's ruined castle, I will honor your wishes."

"And who am I to marry?" she growled.

"Whoever the Horde King sends to take your hand. You will be a good wife to him, one year and one day; that is how long you will endure his touch!"

"You cannot mean it, not after everything they have done to us!"

"You have to pick your battles, daughter. This isn't one I care to wage and neither can you. It's not about what we have already lost which cannot be changed, it's about surviving. With the Horde tied to our line, no other caste would dare trespass against us. I'm tired of fighting with you, with the others who seek to take what our family has created here. For once in your life, do as I have asked of you. Once you have secured a child, you can do whatever you desire. They have given me their word on it."

"Why would they do this now when the war is at their front gates?" she asked, her heart pounding so hard against her chest that it ached. The thunderous beat of it deafened his words as she swallowed the bile that threatened to escape through her lips.

"Because the tithe is due and we cannot pay it. This

was their offer; your hand and all debt this court and your mother's owe, are erased." His words echoed in her ears, the reminder of the last tithe stung, piercing her chest as she watched him age before her eyes.

"My mother's entire court was wiped out by them, or did you forget to remind them of that small detail?"

"Not all of them, daughter," he informed gently as he pushed his blue-white hair away from his bronzed flesh. "You have the bloodline of both of our courts, and the combined heir markings upon your flesh. You are the Queen of the Shadows and the Princess of the Night Court. As the Shadow Court was cleansed, you were protected by the Elite Guards, even if you didn't know it. The new king was younger then, and he spared you what his father intended. You would have been added to his harem, used to secure his hold on this court as he had done to the others. This tithe is different, the world is different, Lilith. Don't fight me on this one, I beg of you."

"It isn't that easy with them," she muttered as her palms sweat and her stomach churned. She was Lilith, born of two royal courts and heir to two thrones. She didn't want to bow willingly to any Horde heathen as long as air filled her lungs.

They didn't deserve the right to her mother's lands, not after they'd beaten her and slaughtered an entire court of people for not paying the tithe. Her father had borrowed and taken from the Shadow Court, leaving them open to attack unknowingly, and her mother had paid for it in blood. And now he expected her to marry some High Fae prince of the Horde? This was straight bullshit.

"They come soon. You are to be here when the moon reaches its zenith in four days. Do you understand? Because even if I have to bind your hands and pluck your tongue from your mouth, you will agree to give the king's brother one year and one day of your life. You're immortal; one year with him is nothing to you."

"Yes, father."

"Lilith, do not do anything to upset them. We cannot continue living as we have been. Not with Winter waging war against us as Summer and Autumn reach for more land."

"We are the court they fear, yet you bow so easily, old man. I am the Queen of Shadows, the only remaining member of the Shadow Court, and I will cower before no man, ever."

"You'd let them destroy this court? Because I assure you, daughter, that is what the price would be if you upset them. They may not wish to do it, but they would because the Horde would demand it of them. So take tonight, and enjoy your freedom while you can. Don't make me force my hand against you."

"And what about what I want?" she asked, her hands shaking as anger took hold of her. "What about what they've done to *my* court?"

"There is no Court of Shadows, but it wasn't only the Horde who destroyed it, Lilith. It was involved in other things, things they shouldn't have been."

"It was the Horde who murdered my court, and his children," she pointed out as she pretended to examine her nails.

"And had they not tried to take down the Horde, he wouldn't have been in the Shadow Court. I understand your anger, trust me. I do. Your mother was the love of my life, my mate. What she did saved us all, and I have never forgiven myself for what happened," he said with a deflating sigh as he stared into the eyes that were so akin to his own.

"If I marry him and secure a child, what then? I'm free?"

"You will be free to remain in that pile of ruins you love so much until my death, at which time you will rule both courts. You have my word on it, Lilith. I may have daughters to spare, but your mother only left me one. You know what you mean to me."

"So much that you are tossing me to the wolves?" she snorted as she crossed her arms and stared up at him.

"I am doing what I have to in order to protect you and this court from history repeating itself. I fear losing you isn't something I wish to endure, daughter. Four days, and then you are to return here to accept the man you will marry."

"Monster, not man," she snapped.

Chapter Two

Asrian stared at Ryder and Synthia, his jaw ticking as they discussed who would be heading off to each corner of the Fae Realm. He'd sworn to do his duty, to collect a wife who they'd chosen, sire an heir upon the wench, and get the fuck out of that realm and back to his own. He'd given that oath long ago, in another lifetime.

Yet here he was, facing his king and queen with his oath being called into play. The entire human world was on the verge of chaos, mortals were losing the war for survival. Faery was waging war against Changelings, and he was being sent off to collect some spoiled brat who he'd wed and bed. *Fucking brilliant.*

"She's the queen of the Shadow Fae and Night Court's chosen heir. It's a good match," Ryder said, even though he didn't believe the shit he was spewing as the others absently listened, knowing their time would come soon enough.

"She's a spoiled little bitch who wants to be

pampered, don't word-fuck me. You and I both know she isn't what I want or need."

"One year, one year to secure an heir and if you have not succeeded, the deal is off. You gave me an oath, Asrian. I don't want this for you, but they need to know we are willing to stand with them or they won't join the fight. We need them at our side, not clawing at us as we prepare for war. Especially with Danu gone," Ryder grumbled as he rubbed his temples in exhaustion.

It wasn't that Asrian didn't think he could collect the little female, or do the deed; it was that he didn't want to deal with a woman who would demand things, or want things from him which he couldn't give. He hadn't expected this oath to come this quickly, and he almost wanted to fork out the gold, harvest, and secure the other items for them to pay the fucking tithe. But that was against the laws of the Fae; no other caste could help another to pay the tithe owed to the Horde. Fucking politics.

"When do we leave?" he asked hesitantly as his brethren watched him. Outside, embers burned, igniting as the world turned to ashes, mirroring his emotions.

"Now; her father is collecting her from the Shadow Court, or what is left of it. She should be at the Night Court already. Asrian, you should know that there is tension you will be faced with; our father made a point of punishing the Night Court as a warning. He also murdered her entire court when they failed to pay the tithe, but also for their part in a plan to remove him from power."

"So my bride is the queen of *nothing*? And she probably hates me and our kind, great," he chuckled. "It just got interesting."

"You will travel with Sinjinn, Cailean, and Tor. I expect you to be on your best behavior and return home with your darling wife already swelling with your child in her womb. The sooner you breed with her, the sooner you can rid yourself of her. If by chance you decide to keep her...make it a mutual thing, understand?" Golden eyes watched him, never faltering as he made sure his every word was heard, and the underlying meaning understood.

"I won't want to keep her. I got a lot of willing women; one spoiled little Queen of Nightmares isn't enough to tame me."

"You're so fucked," Cailean chuckled from behind him, his thickly coiled brands pulsing as he watched through turquoise eyes with thicker black outlining them. "If you don't want her..." he let the offer hang in the air.

"You're betrothed to the Winter Court's princess, fuck-face. Your time will come, and we will see who got off easier. And it's the Queen of Shadows, not Nightmares, that's another court and another bad fucking idea waiting to happen," Torin scoffed as his hazel and brown eyes filled with laughter.

"And you're stuck with Summer, who adores you so much already," Asrian said drolly. "Shadows, Nightmares, same fucking thing. All trouble, all more shit than any of us want to deal with. All about to fuck our world up and ruin the good thing we had going."

"You assholes know I wouldn't do this if there were another way," Ryder injected, his eyes filled with hard steel and resolve. "No one can pay the tithe with Faery failing, and to not collect the debt makes the Horde look weak. Not to mention we are facing a war that may last longer than any of us care to admit. Tithes must be collected, and the courts our father wronged must be righted. Having a bride doesn't end what we have; it just means some of you unlucky fucks are going to be fathers, while some of you may not be. Maybe then you too can be fucking sleep-deprived and worried as fuck every waking minute of the day. In the words of a wise lady, buckle up buttercups, because it's a bumpy ride."

"That's not what I said, Fairy." Synthia glared at him before returning to her gaze to the small child who played on the floor.

"And hopefully you assholes find mates who rut less than this dragon does," Ciara groaned as she rubbed her swollen belly. Fury played on the floor, his tiny hands stretching for his mother as she slid a rattle closer to where he sat. "But if not, be kind to the lass. This shit sucks."

"You love being pregnant," Blane chuckled as his gaze warmed at the sight of his wife. "I hope you guys have an easier time collecting your brides than this one gave me."

"I wasn't willing, asshat, remember?"

"Asshat?" Blane hissed with heat burning in his eyes.

"Asshat," Fury crooned, clapping his hands as Ciara growled.

"Watch your tongue, dragon, or I'll cut it out of your mouth."

"You like my tongue, that's why you keep ending up pregnant."

"Bumper sticker, dragon," Synthia interrupted with a shooing motion of her hands before she knelt down to pick Fury up, returning to her chair with him. "Go read it again, and shoo, both of you. Fury only speaks a few words and most of them are cuss words."

"Asrian taught him the last one, and he says Happy Meal now, who taught him that shit?" Ciara asked with a pointed look.

"Ryder did, and he's king, so he can do as he wants," Synthia smothered a laugh against Fury's dark head as he pulled on her war braids.

"Are you assholes ready?" Sinjinn asked as he fixed the bag of weapons he wore and eyed his brothers. "I still think this isn't the fucking time to be sending the guard off in separate directions, for the record."

"Noted," Zahruk said as he stepped from beside Ryder and handed the brothers scrolls that decreed their bloodline, along with which caste and their place in line for the throne. Alazander had hundreds of children; most of them had been born male, besides Ciara, who they knew of. But they hadn't even begun to search for those who held the Horde's bloodline, and now wasn't the time to start looking. It also wasn't like their father had been kind, and most would be the result of his brutality.

"Let's go aviking!" Tor announced.

"It's not the same." Asrian shoved his brother forward before nodding to the king and queen as they headed outside to the portal.

"It's the same."

"It is not the same. There's no pillaging and burning shit down, which makes it a lot less cool than what the Vikings did."

"*Can* we burn shit down?" Sinjinn asked, and an exasperated sigh came from Ryder.

"You realize they will probably burn half of Faery down pretending to be Vikings now, right?" Synthia laughed as she cradled the toddler.

"Gods save us," Ryder laughed as he shook his head and touched Fury's chubby cheek with his index finger.

"Not even the Gods would touch that one, husband."

Chapter Three

Lilith exploded into the Court of Shadows as chaos and anger filled her veins. How could her father be so cruel? Hadn't they paid enough with the blood of her court to those heathens? So what if the new king had protected her father's court from the same fate? It shouldn't have ever happened. Now she would marry some Horde bastard and stay with him for an entire year?

The ruins shivered as her anger exploded around her. This wasn't happening. Not now, not after everything she'd done to secure a match who would be worthy of rebuilding this court back up to its former glory with. Didn't that mean something to her father? This court had been slaughtered, left in nothing but a pile of ruins and her entire life had been spent rebuilding what the monstrous Horde had done. And now Cade had backed out on her. It was infuriating.

"You're angry," Lara murmured as she stepped from the shadows.

"I'm pissed!" Lilith responded with angry tears filling her eyes. "That bastard!"

"Your father?" she asked hesitantly.

"Yes! He's gone too far this time. He's insane to think he can force this on me."

"He's found a husband?" she guessed, her gentle midnight blue eyes smiling with mischief as she watched her sister.

"Yes!"

"You knew it would come eventually. So, to which caste has he thrown you?"

"To the Horde!" Lilith spat coldly as she watched her sister's complexion pale, losing all color in her face as it sank in.

"No, no, not even he would be so cruel to do that to you. Lilith, why would he do something like that?"

"Because the tithe is once again due, and of course he cannot pay it."

"The Horde is demanding a tithe be paid with the world dying? I thought it had changed, become more understanding of our people. We cannot pay a tithe, and if they demand it from one court, they'll demand it from every court."

"They have. To clear the tithe of the Night and Shadow Court, I will be given to a monster of the Horde for a year and one day."

"We can run, we can hide from them," Lara offered, and Lilith shook her head as she lifted ice blue eyes to the velvet ones that flooded with unshed tears.

"You know that if we run, there will be nothing left of the Night Court, and I cannot allow what happened here to repeat itself. I won't allow them to destroy everything, Lara. You will hold this court, and I will go with him. After one year has passed, I will return and marry Cade if he will keep his deal after this marriage has happened. I promised you we would right this place, that I'd give you a real home. I have not forgotten my promise."

"You will have to sleep with him. The son of a monster who killed our mother! I forbid it."

"You cannot forbid anything," Lilith huffed as she stared into the ruined courtyard of the court she'd chosen to live at. Unlike her father's courtyard, this one was a broken place. It was a hauntingly beautiful ruin of the glorious palace it had been.

"How can you be so calm?" she demanded as she pushed her dark, midnight curls out of her face.

"Because it isn't forever, Lara," she returned as she dipped her aching feet into one of the remaining ponds. "Because we know better than anyone else what happens when you don't pay the tithe. I won't let them take anyone else I love away from me. I don't have to actually sleep with him, either. If he were drunk, he wouldn't know if we had or hadn't done it, right?"

"Men seem to remember taking a maiden's virginity, especially on their marriage bed, Lilith. I mean, maybe if we use our combined magic, we could kill him and tell them he disappeared?"

"That would make us no better than they are. Plus, I've heard rumors that they're unlike the old Horde, that they tend to stick together and are close to one another. It doesn't mean I have to like him or do what is expected of me. I just have to pretend to be subdued, and then disappear for most of the time."

"I think the whole one year and a day is supposed to be spent together to procure an heir, Lilith," she said as she crossed her arms, staring at her sister as she chewed her lip.

"I can't escape this, not without ruining everything we've worked to achieve here."

"I know," Lara agreed as she pushed her dark curls away from her face. "Day is coming, we should sleep. There's nothing we can do to stop this from happening if you won't run. So let's eat and then rest, shall we?" she asked, holding her arm out to indicate they should move inside.

"I feel like I'm drowning, and there's nothing I can do to keep my head above water." Lilith exhaled, following her sister into the ruined castle. "If I run, I doom my bloodline to repeat the same path this one has ended up in. If I run, they would hunt me down and anyone who assisted me. I cannot win, can I?"

"I don't know what bothers me the most. That your father would hand you off to the same monsters that killed our mother, or that you'll have to sleep with *it* to secure a child."

"I realize how babies are created, Lara. But thanks for pointing that out again," she grumbled as her sister used magic to heat the tea, never fully touching the teapot as it tipped to fill both teacups. Lilith reached for the delicate cup, holding her nose above it as she inhaled the rich spices of the tea.

"Maybe I will get lucky, and he won't need to feed for sex, or he'll take other lovers to his bed."

"The Horde is notorious for their feeding habits. There are also rumors that they prefer to be exclusive to the one they wed. This new Horde is dangerous in the way that it is nothing as we've known before. I heard rumors that dragons have married into their folds—dragons!" she exclaimed as she blew on her tea. "Can you imagine them?"

Lilith continued watching her sister. Lara was the one being who she trusted in this world. She was gentle, loving, and mature for her age, considering she was only a mere fifteen years older than Lilith. But Lara had been hidden within the Court of Shadows from her father, from the world really. It was only by the Goddess that Lara had survived the attack on the court. She'd found her here, crying for their mother in the dark of the night. That had been years after the initial attack, and in that time, Lara had been alone.

Liliana had given birth to her a few years before she'd been betrothed to the King of the Night Court. She'd left Lara here, in the protection of her grandfather and King to the Shadow Court, the first target for Alazander when the tithes couldn't be paid in full. Or had there been more than she'd believed? Her father thought there had been.

She'd come here as soon as she was old enough to learn about her mother and what had happened. It was here she'd found the sister she'd never known existed crying, balled up into the fetal position as she pined for anyone to remember she existed. And Lilith hadn't left her since, not even when her father demanded she do so to return to court for good.

"I still think we should run. I know you're afraid of leaving this place, but it's just a place. I'd go with you, and you wouldn't have to marry this…this monster they're sending to murder you."

"Lara, I love you to pieces, but this isn't helping. I doubt the Horde is sending a monster to murder me. My guess is that they're trying to gain control of the lesser courts; marrying the queen of two courts would just be a starting point, don't you think? And while I don't doubt it will be a monster they send, since they only breed them, it won't be one who wants to kill me, because that would be a bad move on his part. I have trained to fight since the moment I could walk; I'm not easy to kill. I came here as a child to escape court politics, to be reminded every day of what they took from me. I rule a dead court, one that was once the largest, scariest court of the lesser Fae. Now nothing more than a court of ruins and rubble, but yet mine to rule all the same."

"With a son from the monsters who laid siege to us," she whispered on a choked sob.

"Stop crying, it doesn't help anything. This is my legacy, my world, and he will be only a moment in time; nothing but a smear in my life that I will erase once I take Cade as my king. A child can be taught to be good, and my child will be part of me too."

"You know I only want what is best for you, and for this court."

"You're my favorite sister," Lilith laughed through the tears in her throat. She pushed away the tears, choking on them as she stared at her sister absently.

"I'm the only sister you actually speak to. Besides, mother died to protect me, and you."

"I wonder what my father would think if he knew about you. He is so full of himself most days, and grandfather and mother hid you so well. I wish I had known her."

"She was like you, fierce and loyal, and brave. She hated the Night Court, and yet she sacrificed her own desires to do her duty. I remember when she brought you home, how jealous I had been that you had her attention, her hair. I look at you, and I see her smiling back at me through you. You are brave for doing this, but that court hasn't even questioned your absence once. You are his heir, and the Queen of Shadows, two titles to two thrones. They should wish for you to grace them with your presence."

"I don't care about being paraded before the court like some symbolic gesture. I know who I am, and I know what I will become. I have you to thank for that since my father refused to train me for war."

"Grandfather believed women to be equal in battle against men. I taught you only what he taught me, and I can only pray to the Goddess that it is enough."

"We should sleep; soon the heathens will be starting their journey to the Night Court, and I will be summoned back to handfast the monster. We must prepare this place for their arrival, because we don't want them to be comfortable here, or want to stay a moment longer than it takes to secure a child."

"You're either brave or insane. I have yet to decide which one you actually are." Lara watched her, smirking as Lilith let the dark curtain of her hair fall into her face to shield her own matching smirk.

"If I were insane, I'd run and think that the Horde couldn't find me."

Chapter Four

Asrian paced outside the king of the Night Court's chambers, listening as the king grumbled about errant children and the early arrival of heathens. What the hell had he expected? For them to actually *walk* here? It was common knowledge that all High Fae could sift, and Faery made it painfully easier on them if they'd been to the location before, which Ryder had strategically picked each place and who would go based on it.

"Is she missing?" Cailean chuckled, his turquoise eyes sparkling with amusement as his platinum hair caught the light and shimmered vibrantly. "You go and scare the little damsel?"

"How the fuck could I have done that, asshole? I was with you. Maybe she saw your pretty face and didn't want to marry a pansy?" he growled as he pushed his fingers through his auburn hair and swore for the millionth time.

"She'd fall in love if she'd seen me first. I figured

I'd stay out of sight and let her hopes not dwindle that it wasn't me she was getting," he said with an exaggerated shrug.

"The King has sent for his daughter, but you weren't expected until tomorrow," the steward said yet again.

The poor man looked like he was ready to piss his pants as he stared up at Asrian's 6'8" frame with open fear. Sinjinn flicked the dagger again, sending it twirling in the air before he caught it, making the man tremble even worse than he'd been.

"Where is she?" he asked as he dismissed his brother, staring at the short little dwarf who couldn't be any taller than four or five feet at most. He watched the worry spread over the little dwarf's face and stifled a laugh of frustration when all he continued to do was peer in awe at Asrian. "Where is the princess?" he asked again.

"At the Court of Shadows, probably hiding from you and your kind," he muttered and then as Asrian watched, he turned an ugly shade of paleness. "I meant…we fear your kind," he said with a shrug. "I'll be honest, your kind only comes to take from us, and the last time they came, they killed our beloved queen. A gentle soul whose only crime was being married to a king who enjoyed lavish things," he explained softly as the color began to return, only in anger as the memories played across his pinched features.

"Our father was a monster, one who not even we care to remember. We are not him, no more than you are responsible for your father, dwarf. The crimes of the past do follow us, but they don't forge the future. We do. My father would never have agreed to a marriage in place of a tithe. Now, would he?"

"No, never. He demanded blood when it could not be paid."

"He did, and we cannot undo that. Yet here we are, willing to take a bride in place of the tithe. That should show you something, should it not?"

"He killed our queen, the princess's mother. I fear she may not see this as a suitable match and rightly so. She prefers the ruins of the Shadow Court to being here, and so is usually there, hiding from everyone she thinks failed her. We should have tried to help them. If you listen at night, you can still hear the screams of the Shadow Court carried on the winds. A reminder to the rest of us what happens when you stand up against those stronger than you."

"As I said, our father was a heartless prick, but that doesn't mean we are created of the same cloth. We've done our best to right his wrongs, but we don't pretend to be anything less than we are. Now, where can I find the Court of Shadows?"

Less than an hour later, the men stood on the edge of the ruins of what was left of the Shadow Court. His father had been a heartless prick to do this, to murder an entire caste of lesser Fae in one tantrum because of something someone else had said they'd done. Asrian remembered this place, remembered the horrors of what had unfolded as he and his brothers had tried to save those they could.

Only a few had made it out alive, and those that had were now hidden and protected by the Horde. This was one of the last places his father had destroyed before his own death. Wiping out entire caste of Fae was unheard of; it unsettled the fragile balance, and there had been no sign of the end to his madness until Ryder, the firstborn son of the Horde King, had challenged him. Not because he'd been ready, but because their father had intended on killing his own sons to ensure the others remained in line.

"Gods, what a fucking mess," Cailean muttered as he wiped his hand over his mouth, letting his eyes settle on the debris that covered the empty courtyard.

"This place used to be beautiful, one of the rare beauties of the lower courts. Great waterfalls once crashed over the edge of that mountain, feeding the moat and lake that surrounded this palace. Father destroyed it, right before he sent the giants to crush the palace. The palace itself was the largest in this realm, towering peaks that touched the clouds. It was one of my favorite places to visit, and then he destroyed it. In one single day, he'd killed the entire court, sparing no one."

Asrian listened as Sinjinn spoke, his words growing thicker as he was lost in another time, another place. He droned on, reminding them all of the past, a time when fear ruled and you either followed what the king said, or you died. These people, this caste had been destroyed for seeking a way to end his reign. They'd been a dark, deadly caste of lesser Fae, one that might have stood a chance if they hadn't been sold out by the Summer Court, who had feared them but also wanted them dead.

A rumble started inside the ruins, and Asrian paused before shifting into his hound form. He started towards the rocks and debris that blocked the main entrance of the ruined palace, sniffing the air as the rich, enticing scent of night blooms lingered, growing stronger as he reached the palace. He'd missed the smell of the night blooms. Once they'd been a sight to behold that glowed iridescently in the night, releasing the seductive scent far into the breeze. Now, they were hard to find and far and in between worlds, misplaced like the people who'd once flourished beside them.

He pawed the ground as his brothers in hound form also paused, scenting her the same moment he had. He lunged as a volley of arrows started towards them, twisting midair as he took his Fae form, taking her to the ground with him as Sinjinn took the other female down as well.

Asrian stared down into eyes the color the brightest full moon, framed by thick, black lashes. The angel who'd tried to kill him and his brothers had the most perfect, full lips and a heart-shaped face. Her eyes filled with murder as they watched his slow perusal of her features. Midnight curls pooled around her body, appearing of the softest silk that his fingers itched to trail through. He swallowed hard, audibly as he lifted some of his weight from her, moving his green gaze to where the bow sat, discarded.

"I'm here for Lilith," he uttered thickly, not immune to the beauty who glared up at him.

"And you would be, heathen?" she hissed.

"Asrian, son of Alazander," he replied softly before he bent his nose down against the soft, creamy perfection of her neck and inhaled deeply of the night bloom that seemed to cling to her flesh. "Her betrothed."

"Do you mind getting off of me?" she hissed again thickly as she pushed against him. He slowly lifted, pushing the bow away from her as she rose to her dainty feet. Asrian rose with her, staring down at her where she barely reached his chest. She was childlike, but her curves left no doubt that she was all woman.

She was tiny, dainty, and yet he could see the fire burning in her eyes along with the pain he sensed she held in check, barely. It called to the demon inside of him, the one that craved pain and the need to feed from it.

"You can stop staring at me, asshole," she chided as she turned those icy blue eyes away from him to stare at Sinjinn, who was just now helping the other female up from where he'd taken her to the ground. "Is this how heathens retrieve their brides?" she snapped crossly, her arms tight against her sides as she peered around, as if searching for her bow.

"No, normally we show up, throw them over our shoulders and spank that ass," Cailean offered amusedly as he stared at her. "If you want, sugar, I can oblige and show you how we *heathens* like to get down."

"You think that's cute? How about I cut those lips off and use them to kiss your own arse with?"

"Hey," he said, holding up his hands in surrender. "You want to kiss my ass, I'll let you. But trust me, these lips are way more useful where they are."

"Enough," Asrian snapped as he pinched the bridge of his nose. "I came for Lilith. I don't have time to sit and split hairs with you. Which one is the woman I am to handfast with?" he asked, and hell if he wasn't praying it was the blue-eyed one with fire burning in her veins. He wasn't even sure if they were actually blue, or just tinted such, but then he didn't care either way. It was the fire burning in her that lured him to her, the pain she hid that he wanted.

"I am Lilith, you oaf," she admitted as she turned those eyes in his direction, and the shadows seemed to creep towards them, eerily. "I was told you wouldn't arrive until tomorrow."

"Well I'm here now, so let's go. I have no intention of being here any longer than I have to be."

"Don't like what you did to the place?" she asked pointedly, her eyes daring him to say no.

"I liked it before my prick of a father destroyed it, lady," he admitted and watched as her fight deflated, as if she'd expected him to say something else. "We didn't want to destroy it, but then when the Horde King says or else, you do what he says."

"And the new one? He said jump and you did so? Impressive, you're a fucking lap dog, do you say *woof* too? I've always wanted a dog."

"Careful, I enjoy fighting but I prefer fucking, and you're about to be my wife to enjoy for a year. You choose what happens between us. I can be your fucking fairytale or I can be your fucking nightmare. That choice is yours, princess."

Chapter Five

Lilith watched as the Neanderthal continually paced outside the ornamented doors of the Night Court. This was the monster she was to marry and spend an entire year of her life with? He was a giant! She wasn't sure what she had expected, but it hadn't been him. He was incredibly tall, forcing her neck to careen to look up and glare at him. His skin was bronzed, kissed by the Gods as if he spent endless days bathing in the sun without worry. The gentle scent of wood and outdoors clung to him, tickling her nose as he passed by her, endlessly pacing. His hair was red, a mixture of auburn and other shades that only enhanced his male beauty.

Of all the beasts she'd expected, it hadn't ever occurred to her that he would be pleasant to look upon. She liked him less for that fact. He hadn't spoken much, but the other male with him had filled the awkward silence with flirting endlessly with the women who served the court. His tri-colored eyes seem to hesitate as they landed on her, quickly moving away as if he didn't care to look longer than was polite.

"You have not started repairs in the Court of Shadows, why?" the darker haired Fae asked. Sinjinn, wasn't that what he'd told Lara his name was?

"We do not have the power of glamouring it back to its former glory after your kind destroyed it," she answered sharply, her tone a mixture of anger and hate.

"No, you wouldn't, but with Asrian with you, it would be easy enough to remake it as you wish it to be. Our kind does have some useful abilities, princess."

She stared at him, wondering if he actually meant it or if he was only saying what he thought she wanted to hear. It would be just like them, to offer empty promises. She had prayed to the Goddess, begging her or anyone listening to right the wrongs of the past, to bring back the power and beauty of the Palace of Shadows so she could see it. She had never gotten to see what it had looked like before it had been destroyed, and had only the word of others to imagine it through.

"If I agree to this, maybe," she said softly, her hand skimming against the daggers hidden in the folds of the gown she wore. She'd taken her time preparing to travel here, forcing the men to wait among the rubble as she'd slowly readied herself. The dress she wore was ice blue, with a deep V-line that exposed more curves than she'd intended it to. It had tulle ruffles that flowed delicately to the floor, covering the thin heels she'd selected for this occasion. Her hair had been piled into a work of magic, with curls escaping it to frame her heart-shaped face. Platinum bands covered her biceps, as a crown of black jewels sat atop her head. Beneath she wore nothing, no sexy garment, no enhancement to push up her breasts as the other ladies of court wore.

"You don't want this, do you?" Sinjinn asked pointedly, not bothering with proper court etiquette.

"Would it matter if I said I didn't?" she asked, her eyes not missing the slight flinch or tick in his jaw as he quickly hid his reaction.

"No, it would change nothing that is happening. Unfortunately, your father isn't able to pay the tithe demanded of him or this court. He was given a year past what was asked, and still has been unable to pay the tithe."

She stared into his tri-colored eyes, watching as the green seafoam ate away at the outer chocolate brown ring. His hair was pulled back, sleek and not a single strand out of place as he slowly took her dress in. "The tithe is unjustly requested. No one can pay what is needed as the world doesn't offer what it once did. Crops are failing as more and more portals appear from the human realm into this one. What goods we do have are used to barter to keep the people of the land from starving. How can you expect to ask it of us, when you and your kind are the bane of the infection that grows in this world," she paused, as if she realized too late who she was arguing her point with. "And even if this buys us time, it will never be enough for you or your kind. You take from us, the lesser Fae, to feed the High Fae and their needs. We are nothing to you, nor will we ever be."

"I don't think you understand the why of it, or who really brought this blight upon us. We didn't ask for war, nor did we condone what our father did to this world. Life isn't black and white, and we who live in the grey part of it have to choose which path we take. My father, that murderous bastard treated his own children worse than any other people, even the ones he sought to destroy." Sinnjinn's eyes glowed as his fingers ignited, as if the memory was too much, or too dark to endure.

"Murderous bastard," Cailean muttered as a visible tremor rushed through him. He pushed his hands through his thick, platinum hair as turquoise eyes slowly slid from Asrian to Sinjinn, then settled on Lilith with a languidness that spoke volumes. "Wish we could bring him back just to watch him die again and again."

"He was your father," she uttered coldly.

"He was our king, our torturer, and the monster who dictated what we were allowed to do, and what happened if we didn't follow his orders. A father protects his children; ours tormented and used us as his personal assassins. Those who didn't follow his rules died. End of fucking discussion," Asrian growled, his eyes green and glowing as something cold and ancient shone from within them.

The doors swung open, revealing guards who waited on either side of the entrance to lead the small party to the king and his throne. Lilith straightened her shoulders and her resolve as she moved to stand beside the giant she was about to marry. She would follow through with this marriage of horror to save this court, one who held no love for her.

That wasn't true; a few did actually like her because of whom and what her mother had done. It was a legendary move she wished to the Goddess hadn't been required, but that and nothing else she did would change the hands of time. And here she was, the daughter of the martyr making another sacrifice to the Horde for this court.

Once they paused in front of her father, she bowed at the waist before lifting, glancing sideways as the giant stared down her father. She turned, taking in what he must see. Her father was young for being king; even at three centuries in age, he was one of the newest royalties in the lesser courts, save her. She was the youngest queen in history, becoming the Queen of Shadows when still unable to make words work from her dainty lips. But then the entire court had been wiped out minus Lara and herself, and Lara's father had been a human.

"I see you found your bride," her father noted, his ice blue eyes slowly holding Lilith's in silent rebuke.

"She was where the steward said she would be. She welcomed us splendidly," he said, and Lilith had to force her eyes from rounding in shock.

It was widely known that the High Fae couldn't lie and yet hadn't he just done so? No, he'd played with words, making her father believe she'd been subservient to his arrival, instead of the truth which was that she'd tried to murder them all. Albeit failing miserably which was probably for the best all things considered.

"Did she? I find that hard to believe as my Lilith is quite skilled with weapons and doesn't take kindly to strangers stumbling into her ruins."

"I stand by what I said, unless you are challenging it as truth?" Asrian growled, his chest reverberating with the threat.

She turned, taking in the way he held himself, prepared to defend his person should the need arise, yet to an untrained eye, he looked relaxed. He stood straight, confident before a king known for twisting creatures apart with his bare hands; however there was not a single ounce of fear showing from any of the Horde who had entered this court.

"I would never question your word. I only meant that she tends to need a firm hand. She is wild and untamed, which I am sure you'll discover for yourself soon enough."

"She's beautiful, and more than I expected. I don't intend to remain here longer than is necessary, so if we could proceed with the ceremony?"

"Yes, of course. I have had a dinner prepared as well," the king stated.

"After visiting your lands, don't you think it would be wiser to invite the people starving outside the gates to your city inside to eat the meal, rather than the ones who look as if they could miss a meal or ten? We will stay for the dinner, and those starving outside shall be invited in." Asrian watched the king, his eyes burning with anger as the kings face mottled, and turned red.

"That is unheard of! It's outrageous to even consider letting peasants inside to eat with royalty." The king waved his hand as if the conversation was finished.

"I insist," Asrian continued, placing his hand on his sword that had remained on his hip.

"In these lands, I am king."

"You are king because we allow it. Your people are starving, and yet the ones in this room are grotesquely overfed. Either invite them in to feast or send the meal out to them. A king who doesn't protect or care for his people shouldn't expect to remain king for very much longer. You have impressed my brother, the King of the Horde, but not me. You sit in here, bathed in gold and fine jewels while people starve right outside your gates. Your own staff is underfed, proving you are the wrong choice for king. Decide, and I will decide which tale I bring back to the king who supported your claim for this throne before he was the actual king. You may have forgotten how you rose to power, but we have not."

"Have the feast placed outside the gates, feed the people the dinner I had prepared for my daughter and her new husband," he grumbled as he stared at Asrian, who hadn't flinched under his dark stare. "You will be leaving directly after the ceremony?"

"I will; the only reason we have even come is for you to see her handed off to the Horde. The next tithe will be paid, or a new king will be crowned."

"You don't have that power!"

"We have the Goddess of Faery on our side, do you?" Sinjinn chuckled as Lilith's eyes swung to his.

Holy shit!

Chapter Six

The ride back to the Court of Shadows was long and filled with silence. Lilith had pilfered bread and meat, along with cheese for supper. It wasn't that she hadn't respected what Asrian had done for her people, but she'd actually been starving for the meal which would have been a welcome distraction. Instead, she was now snacking nervously as he watched her.

A fire had been lit by Lara, who had prepared the one bedroom that they'd been sharing. Lara would now be sleeping under the stars while she and Asrian shared the sister's bedroom which had once belonged to their mother.

"Are you warm enough?" he asked, his back still to her as he stroked the fire to a beautiful mixture of red and orange flames.

"Yes," she answered as she shivered, trembling against what she knew was coming. Something she had no idea how to deal with, or even how it occurred since she'd skipped over that day with her handmaiden, and hadn't gone back since. "I don't…I'm not sure how this next part works," she continued hesitantly.

"Fucking?" he chuckled.

"You don't have to be so crude," she hissed as she stood and moved to the furthest wall away from him. She rubbed her bare arms, wishing she'd worn the long-sleeved dress of her mother's instead of the shorter-sleeved one she'd chosen.

"You're not that young," he pointed out crossly. When she continued to peer up at him, he swore beneath his breath. "I'm going to break his fucking nose for this."

"Whose nose?" she asked when he just continued to stare at her.

"Ryder's, he knows I'm not interested in uncharted territories."

"He is your king and the king of the entire Horde. You would be so careless with your life?"

"You think us monsters, but he isn't like that. He's… kind, and yet deadly enough to hold his title because of what he holds inside of him. Here, drink this," he said as he poured wine into a glass and extended it to her.

She accepted it, sipping at it generously as she stared at the bed that sat in the middle of the room. It had silver sheets with the petals of the night blooms spread out over it. Lara knew the flowers would calm Lilith, or should have. Considering she was about to do the last thing she wanted to with this giant, nothing short of valerian roots dipped in the Fairy Pools themselves would calm her pounding heart and nerves.

She tipped the glass up and then held it out for more, watching the red liquid as it flowed into the glass. Why was she so damn nervous? She just had to survive this deed once and be done with it and him, right? Her kind was notoriously fertile, but his kind wasn't...she stared at him from beneath her lashes as he removed his shirt, revealing nicks and gashes that at one time had been horrid wounds.

"Ouch," she uttered without thinking. How many of those wounds had her people given him? Plenty, she hoped.

"My father's talented with a blade, or he was," he explained, and she felt her face scrunching up at his answer.

"Surely you got that from fighting people who couldn't defend themselves," she hissed, and then realized how stupid her own words sounded as they left her lips.

"I did what I did to survive him," he returned sharply. "Your people fought hard, but not nearly as hard as we had to in order to survive being his children. Remove the dress, Lilith. Lay down with me," he growled.

"You and your people slaughtered mine, and now I am to be your prize."

"And what a beautiful prize you are, princess. One fit for a king."

She blushed, feeling the heat as it flooded her cheeks and then he stepped closer, and she darted backwards, slamming her back against the stone wall she'd rebuilt with her bare hands. He chuckled as he slowly made his way to where she was backed against it, caging her in with his hands barring her escape. His mouth lowered, drifting towards hers as he tasted her mouth slowly.

"You're trembling; do I scare or excite you, Lilith?"

he questioned before he sucked her full, plump lip between his teeth and held it gingerly before releasing it. A soft moan exploded from her lips as a foreign sensation sent sparks sailing through her, igniting something white-hot in her belly.

"I don't like you, or what you are," she replied absently as she lifted her mouth for more, needing to know what that sensation had been. "I will do this for them, the starving people who already suffer because of the world and because I cannot change that. I can stop your kind from invading and doing to that court what was done to this one."

"Noble, but stupid," he chuckled heatedly. The scent of wine mingling with masculinity had her head swimming in emotions she wasn't sure how to process. She'd expected to hate him, and yet he was smooth, so fucking smooth, and said all the right things at the same moment she wanted to hurl an argument at him. "Your father was so quick to throw you at us, the Queen of Shadows, and Princess of the Night Court. Born and bred of pureblooded parents, a Queen of the Courts. Yet I get here, and I found you," he murmured as he kissed her cheek softly. "Some fucking maiden who stares at me like I'm a fucking monster and hates my guts," he said amusedly. "And she's the most beautiful thing I think I've ever laid my bastard eyes upon. You don't deserve to suffer this, so do me a fucking favor; you can fill the wine, and when we've finished drinking it, we will sleep."

"What?" she uttered softly, questioningly.

"What I mean is this: You don't want this, and I have no intention of forcing it on you. I'm a bastard, but

I'm not that much of one."

"No, no, you will finish this, and when you report back to your king, it will be with the truth, word player. I will not chance losing my court. Not again, so you will do what is expected, and now!" Panic threatened to consume her at the idea of him turning her down, what it could mean for her people.

"Gods, woman, which is it? You don't want me, yet you demand I fuck you, and yet you loathe me, you hate everything I fucking stand for. You want this? Down the wine, strip your delicate little ass naked, and we'll play this game. I'll give you a fucking monster."

She swallowed hard at the anger that burned in his eyes, the glow that lit them from within. Power ignited in the room and slithered over her flesh as he watched her lift the shaking glass to her mouth, downing the wine in a single gulp. She pushed the cup out in front of her, watching as he filled it once more, and she did it again and again until her nerves no longer had her trembling with fear or her own idiocy.

He'd offered her a way out, but what if he was like the others and decided to admit they hadn't completed their vows? She couldn't chance it, not with who he had ties to. Not with so much riding on her doing this to save her people.

She lit the candles in the room, using her power to burn them and extinguish the other light that would allow him to see the blush spreading through her system. Next, she slowly reached behind her with trembling fingers as she began to undress, but his hands rested over hers, stalling her clumsy attempt to strip.

His hands were steady as he pushed hers away,

using his fingers to trail over her naked shoulder before his heated mouth skimmed it, following the same dangerous path. Her skin pebbled as he kissed his way to the crease of her neck, slowly working his way to her ear before he nipped the lobe, pulling on it as a deep rumble escaped his lips.

Asrian's fingers worked the zipper of the dress, carefully removing it before letting it pool at her feet. He lifted his mouth, turning her to face him as his hands slid down her sides, stopping at her hips. He lowered his mouth to hers, claiming it in a jarring kiss that sent a shockwave pulsing through her entire body. She groaned, pushing her tongue into the depths of his mouth as she reached up, hooking her hands around his neck.

The taste of wine and male hit her, buckling her knees as he kept her adrift in the sea of passion that threatened to consume her. The last time she'd kissed someone, there hadn't been this heat. Cade's stolen kisses hadn't done this to her senses. He hadn't made her feel as if she was adrift in a storm, crashing from one wave to the next with a single kiss.

Asrian lifted her, and absently she wrapped her legs around him, holding on as he moved them towards the bed. A single thought screamed through her mind, *He was her enemy*. So why was she throwing herself at him again? Why did she never want his mouth to leave hers?

She'd lost her ever-loving shit; that was what was happening, right? She felt her body lowering, and then he pulled away from her, standing back up as he deftly worked the jeans he wore. Heathen, he hadn't even dressed up for their handfasting, and it would have merely taken a single thought to manage it, unlike her.

His cock sprung free, and she sat up, her eyes watching as it bounced proudly before her. Oh hell, that thing was an actual monster. She now understood why he'd said he'd give her a monster.

"Um…" she hesitated as she lifted her ice blue gaze to his, and found glowing green orbs of lust staring back. High Fae, High fucking Fae…and she'd forced the issue.

"No, not happening now," he warned as he bent between her legs and pulled them apart before settling there. He gazed down at her alabaster flesh, as white as the snow when it fell at the beginning of the year. His hands lowered, encircling her hips as he adjusted her body and then stared at her thinness.

She was like a branch, a thin, delicate branch and he a massive oak tree, unbending, while she, on the other hand, could easily be snapped. Thick coils of muscles tensed on his stomach, rippling with strength as he released her, and lowered his mouth to rain kisses down her smooth belly. It was intoxicating, more so than the wine she'd downed to quiet the nerves.

His mouth was magic, spelled by Merlin to lower her defenses and sneak past them. He continued until his mouth touched her clitoris and her back arched as her hands slid through his hair, pulling him away from her as a blush flooded her cheeks as apprehension shot through her.

"What are you doing?" she demanded as a roguish smirk danced on his lips as the glow in his eerie eyes intensified. "You can't eat me, I'm not food."

"You're so fucking pure the bards could sing ballads

about it," he murmured before his mouth lowered again, uncaring that she yanked at his hair to keep him from biting her flesh...and then his tongue pushed through her slick folds, and all coherent thought left her.

She moaned loudly as she parted her legs, giving him further room to work with. Her body hummed with an electrical current that threatened to bring the castle ruins down onto their heads. Lilith hadn't ever imagined pleasure before, let alone this all-consuming pleasure his mouth was doing to her body. A ball of white-hot energy built in her belly and she lessened her hold on his hair as he worked her pussy, licking it as she grew heated until she thought she'd turn to embers and burn up.

Asrian's finger pushed into her body without his mouth leaving her, but it felt foreign, wrong. She wiggled her bottom, adjusting to the feeling until he added another. Her body was slick with heat, and sweat built between her breasts and her nape. That white-hot ball in her belly grew and grew until she was screaming as everything exploded and went wrong.

Tears slid down her cheeks, her body trembled, continuing as he climbed up to wipe them away with his thumbs. His mouth claimed hers hungrily, stealing away the embarrassment of her body's strange reaction to his. She felt him pushing against her opening and cried out as he pushed his body against hers, battering past her innocence.

Pain exploded as her heartbeat thundered in her ears. He slowed, stalling as he stared down into her tear-filled gaze. His mouth lowered, kissing the tears away as his brands ignited, his hips rocked, and the pain was replaced with that foreign fullness. Her body clenched against his and her hands found his shoulders, holding onto him as he started to move in a steady rhythm. He filled her painfully full until it burned and ached. Moments passed and yet he continued, his mouth claiming hers as he kissed her gently, letting her guide his pace.

Once the pain was a dull ache, she rolled them, lifting her body to tower over his as she stared down into his hungry glowing green gaze. Her hands slowly lowered, tracing the smooth path to his muscles, exploring the warrior beneath her as her hips began to move, seeking that earth-shattering pleasure his fingers had given her moments ago.

Asrian reached up, cupping her full breasts in his hands as he explored her body with wonder in gaze, as if he couldn't believe she was real. His mouth lifted which jostled his hips and sent his thick cock deeper, forcing a cry of pain to escape her lips.

He rolled them, lifting her knees until they were against her shoulders. Deep, he was so fucking deep that she could feel him against her womb. His auburn head dropped, and his tongue traced a path over one pebbled nipple before mimicking the action with the other. He sucked it between his teeth, letting them scrape against it for maximum effect. She felt him moving again, even though he had yet to release her breasts with his hungry mouth.

Her body started to heat once more, that white-hot ball inside her belly building as he worked her pussy and kissed her breasts before his hand slid between them, working her clit until she was bucking against his intrusion, uncertain if she'd survive the magnitude of the storm he was creating. All at once, he jerked and growled as it hit, her body a never-ending ball of trembling need that left her visibly shaking against his massive frame.

"Gods, woman," he uttered as he stared down at the hot, disheveled mess he'd created. "You're fucking perfect, and mine."

"I am not yours, not any longer than a year and a day, heathen," she whispered as she pushed him away, embarrassment at her wanton behavior sneaking up as she replayed her actions. These beings had murdered her mother and yet here she was, screaming like a wanton nymph beneath him. "Get off of me."

"You wanted this, not me," he grumbled as he rolled from her body, swiftly moving to retrieve his clothing. He didn't put them on; instead, he tossed them into the fire and dressed with magic, his glamour effortlessly allowing him a smooth exit as she remained in bed, fighting traitorous tears as her actions and behavior swallowed her whole.

How could she have liked it that much? She'd found it a chore to kiss Cade, and yet with Asrian, his kiss had consumed her, easing her nervousness as surely as any wine could. One year and one day, and after that, she'd never see him again. She sent a prayer to the heavens, asking the Goddesses to ensure that when the time came, it was an easy break from the heathen she'd just found pleasure from.

Chapter Seven

Lilith stretched in bed, hating the subtle reminder of the night before as muscles she hadn't even known could hurt ached and burned. It took her longer than usual to move from the bed, and as she did, she cocked her head and listened. Silence greeted her, and she smiled; maybe she'd been bipolar enough to send his ass running for the hills.

She slipped into the bath, dressing in a soft white maxi dress with slits up to the hip. She strapped her weapons on, slinging her bow over her shoulder before attaching the quiver full of arrows, and adjusting the wristband on her arms. Without another thought, she exited her bedroom and stopped dead in her tracks.

Where there should have been a pile of rubble was a wall, which attached to a hallway. She put her palm flat against it and pushed hard, noting the sturdiness of it before she followed the corridor down to a fork that led in three different directions. She looked between them slowly before turning in the direction from which she'd come. The hell? She was lost in her own freaking palace. It had never had walls since she'd found the damn thing!

After countless wrong turns and endless exploring, she reached a large room where voices were laughing, talking, and men, a lot more men than had been here last night. She stalled slowly, leaning against the wall as she eavesdropped on Asrian discussing his plans to right the outside courtyard.

Angry tears swam in her vision as all her own plans for this place went out the door. Her people had built it up from the ground, making it the largest, strongest court in the history of the lesser Fae, and here this insignificant prick was designing it as if he owned the place? No fucking farting fairy's chance.

She stepped into the room, noting the chatter come to silence as she stared at the man who sat on a throne of swirling dark eddies. His body fit it perfectly, as if it had been created for him. She stalked closer, staring at the men who all watched her with a look of curiosity.

"The fucking fairy farting dwarves do you think you're doing, heathen?" she demanded, and the men barked in laughter, which only made her even madder. "This is my palace, my kingdom! You don't get to destroy it and then remake it as you wish!"

"Lilith, this is the exact palace that was here before our father rendered it to nothing more than a pile of rubble. I believe the words you are looking for are *thank you, my king*." Asrian stared down at her, daring her to say something.

"One year and one day, then I am the queen, and you're gone, heathen king," she hissed before she spun on her heel and marched from the room. She couldn't even argue if it was an exact match because he and his family had stolen it from her.

"Well, congrats, she didn't swoon on your cock and bow down. I guess I'm the better lover after all," Tor chuckled.

"She's got more mood swings than Alice in fucking Wonderland on acid. One minute she's cold, the next she's hot. Her mood swings make Ciara look normal. Marriage fucking sucks. How the hell does Ryder make it look so easy?" Asrian groaned as he rubbed his temples.

"Um, did you miss the whole Synthia beating him up or driving him insane part? Anything worth having isn't going to be easy to get. She's a hellcat, so take her claws from her. Make her want us to be here, ask her what she wants. We fixed the castle, but we can't fill it with her people. We can't bring the dead back, nor can we expect these beings to forgive us easily. Respect is earned, not given," Sinjinn said solemnly.

"I don't understand women. I mean, I gave her an escape. I gave her an out to sleeping with me, and she told me no. She liked it, and the moment it ended, she hated me again." He scratched his head as he stared at the door she'd escaped through.

"Maybe she just didn't like you that much? I can try, I mean, she's got a nice body. I have been working on my wooing skills too," Cailean offered, and Asrian turned his head slowly, leveling him with a lethal stare. "Hey, what's the harm in it? And if in a few months she gives birth to a blonde little badass, he'll be mine. No one the wiser until then, right?"

A Demon's Plaything

Asrian rose from the throne, stepping down to start after the woman who seemed immune to his charms. Sure, he wasn't the wooing type, he wasn't even sure he had a fucking type other than willing and ready, but this was his wife.

He passed through several empty hallways and more empty rooms before he heard it: the sound of arrows cutting through the air, thumping against a target in the distance. Once outside, he leaned against the wall, watching as she hit the mark every time, each arrow cutting through the next as she let her anger out with every shot. Well look at that, she was a little badass with a bow. They'd been lucky she hadn't given them a fight because while it may not have killed them, it wouldn't have been pleasant.

He cocked his head again, listening to the silence of the palace and then watched as she did the same. Her shoulders slumped as she sat the quiver and bow aside and stared up at the high castle walls, glaring at the Horde banister as she set eyes on it. Those expressive eyes of hers did little to hide her anger—or pleasure for that matter.

Her body was a haven, one he'd been lost in but her pain? It was fucking addictive. Not as overpowering as Synthia or Lena's, but more soothing, like coming home. He crossed his arms and watched her, noting the way she stood, ready to fight. Trained for war, and yet so fucking delicate and dainty that an attacker wouldn't take her seriously, which would be a huge fucking mistake. They should, the way she stood, the way she used the bow, self-taught. Warriors created from the need to survive were deadly. He'd been trained since the moment he could stand up, but Lilith trained herself, and no one could be harsher on someone than themselves.

Asrian watched as she neared the wall, shucking off her shoes as she leapt against it, climbing it as he watched. What the fuck? She climbed as one who had centuries of training; fearless immortals wouldn't try to scale a castle barehanded, and yet here she was, in all her fucking glory doing just that.

Once she reached the top, she ripped the banner down, watching as it drifted to the ground. Their eyes locked and she smirked; confidence was fucking sexy, but confidence and an outright fucking challenge?

Game on, little warrior.

Chapter Eight

Lara watched her, unnervingly so.
Her fingers drummed on the table, a brand new table they'd created from magic. Together they sat in an empty hall, filled with the echoes of the dead and yet no sound at all. She wanted to lay waste to it, to render it back to rubble. To the beautifully haunting ruins that mirrored her soul. But nope, he'd decided he was in charge and the king of it, and waltzed right in and fucking took over the place.

"You ladies hungry?" Sinjinn asked as he entered the hall, a steaming platter of food in his hands. She turned, eyeing it before she dismissed him.

According to Lara, it was exactly as it had been before it had been destroyed. That meant they'd been here when it had happened, because things had been remodeled right before they'd attacked, and no one outside the court had been allowed into the palace. Which also meant she'd fucked someone responsible for murdering her family.

"I'm famished," Lara said with a wide smile as the food was set down in front of her.

"My appetite just soured. I'm going hunting."

"We have enough meat to last a few days," Sinjinn offered carefully.

"I'm not going hunting for food," she hissed, her lips curving into a sexy smirk. "I'm hunting monsters that slither into my lands and take things that don't belong to them." She stared at him in open challenge as the other men waltzed in, stopping at the tense scene before them.

"And who would that be?" he asked.

"Anything stupid enough to fucking try me," she answered coldly as she pushed past him and started to leave the room to retrieve her quiver and bow.

"What the fuck is your problem?" Asrian demanded as he stepped in front of her.

"My problem? I didn't have a fucking problem until you showed up here and messed my life up! You had no right to fix the castle!"

"It's my castle now too until I choose otherwise!" he shouted back as he balled his fists at his sides.

"It's not your dead screaming at you! It's not you who has to hear the silence and know they're gone. That every one of them died fighting against monsters like you! It's a fucking reminder that we lost and that you and your people took them away. You murdered children and women and left their corpses here to rot like trash. Do you know who got to clean it up? We did, two fucking kids who had nothing and no one left! So if you're expecting a thank you, hold your fucking breath while you wait, heathen king!" She lunged, but not for his waist; instead, she dove for his legs, twisting her body around them and taking him to the floor before she flipped to her feet and stared down at where the giant lay, baffled.

She exploded into darkness, becoming night and shadows as she escaped the room in an ebb of anger and grief. She surged to a semi-solid form a few feet away from him and stared at him, her body never fully becoming solid as she waited for him to attack her. Her eyes glowed from within, a reminder that she'd used her power outside of night, and without the protection of the shadows. Only stronger of the lesser Fae could use powers without a direct link to their court, and she'd had to be strong. Lilith had never felt more alone than when she was surrounded by the Night Court, lost in a wave of endless people who suffered without being able to end their pain.

"I'm not your enemy, Lilith." Asrian stared her down, unflinching as he let his own power fill the room. "I won't continue to apologize for what happened here because words mean nothing, less than nothing. You think you're the only one who lost people because of him? Blane and the dragons lost thousands the same as you have lost here, and yet he can forgive. Our father didn't ask our permission, nor would it have made a difference, but your court isn't all gone. Some were allowed to escape. Some of them we hid, and they are still alive."

"You think I'm going to buy your lies? I know my people are gone because if they weren't, I'd feel them. I'd feel the call to them."

"Then let us show you them, all of them. Come

with us, we can prove it." Sinjinn stepped closer, slowly closing the distance between himself and Asrian. "There's a village, deep in the Hidden Realm. It's spelled to protect those who we hid within the walls. We had no plans of genocide, and after the dragons were slaughtered, we took steps to protect people. I rebuilt your caste, Lilith. Me, I was here when it fell, when your people fell, not Asrian. Asrian was still cleaning up another mess our father had made. He has none of your blood on his hands, and if he had, Ryder wouldn't have chosen him to be here with you, or to marry you."

"I would feel them, and I feel nothing. I'm the heir, I hold the bloodline."

"What if I did too?" Lara asked, and Lilith's head snapped in her direction. "If I tell you, you have to promise it changes nothing between us. Promise me?"

"Your father was human, Lara. A mere human male who wandered into mother's garden long ago."

"My father raped our mother and left her on the stairs of this very castle. A monster, one who collected a pound of flesh for the tithe that wasn't paid," she whispered. Lilith expelled a breath as she stared at Lara as if she'd grown another head. "He took her away for months, abusing her until he'd extracted his payment, and when he'd finished, he left her pregnant and soiled on her father's stairs. I didn't tell you because when you showed up, I wasn't alone anymore. I'd found you, and you, you hated them so very much. You were my sister, my blood. I'd thought I had lost everyone, and then you walked in and just like that, I wasn't alone anymore. So I hid what I was, and we began cleaning up the remains that I couldn't stomach to alone, you and I, Lilith, you and I."

"Shut your mouth," Lilith cried. "Don't say it."

"I don't have to, because you know what I am."

"No, no you can't be because that would make you one of them!"

"I'm still your sister. I'm still the girl who braids your hair at night and tells you stories of our mother."

"That's why you couldn't come to the Court of Night," Lilith said as she covered her mouth with her arm, smothering her scream of rage. "That's why they hid you here?"

"This was the only place I was safe from his reach until he came and destroyed it. Then I was alone, until you. I couldn't be with Mother, because what I was couldn't be hidden until I Transitioned, but once I had, I learned to hide what I am."

"Oh my Gods, did you fuck your sister?" Tor exclaimed, forcing every eye to turn in his direction.

"Lilith isn't your father's child, only I am," Lara admitted as Lilith stumbled backwards, turning into darkness as Lara reached for her. "Lilith, please!"

"You lied to me, about everything!"

"I couldn't tell you what I was, I couldn't tell anyone." Lara turned, staring up at where Lilith now stood in the rafters. She vanished into a dark storm cloud and slipped out of the palace into the night.

"You're one of them. That's why you alone survived this attack; because the Horde doesn't kill their own, especially women."

"I'm alive because one of them pushed me out a window into the pond behind the castle, protecting me from Alazander and his wrath. I'd have died with them if he hadn't! I was spared because not all of them wanted us dead; because some of them did as they are telling you. You can't keep living with the ghost of the past. You're becoming one of them, Lilith. We both have been, day and night, we sit in the ruins and try to rebuild it, but we are the only ones here. There can be no court without people, and no matter what we do or fix, that won't change. Let them show us, let them take us to our people, please!"

Lilith turned into shadows and slipped from the castle, hiding from the hurt and pain of betrayal. The castle rumbled with it, trembling as she exploded into the night, away from those who had created the endless betrayal and pain she now felt. Her own sister was one of them, the girl who had held her at night, whispering that the ghost of the castle they lay within would forgive them for moving on, for continuing living even though they no longer did. Yeah, right. Everyone was a liar, a fucking coward and liar who said whatever it took to get what they wanted, and she was finished with it all.

Chapter Nine

Lilith turned from shadows to her true form on the rocks of the bay that stood on the edge of Nightmare Bay. Her scream was smothered by the crashing waves of the ocean. Tears stung her eyes as salt water splashed, sprayed her where she faced the dangerous sea that raged, mirroring the emotions that crushed the air from her lungs.

Thunder clapped loudly above her as she lifted her face to the rain that began, slowly drizzling before it let loose, pounding anything crazy enough to be outside during a storm in Faery.

Her hair clung heavy against her flesh, ice cold as the storm turned from a spring drizzle to a beautiful, chaotic storm that howled, sending a shower of small ice balls pounding against the ocean's waves.

How could Lara have kept this from her? Did she think it would have changed how Lilith felt? They'd been alone, mourning their mother and their people together. It did explain the one question Lilith had always pondered in silence over: How had Lara survived and been spared when no one else had? Because she'd been one of them, and they'd seen it.

Betrayal stung, but this one would leave a mark that wouldn't soon heal. Did it change how she felt about her sister? No, she was her sister, but she also wouldn't trust her as quickly as she had before. She swallowed another scream, wiping away at the hot, angry tears that flowed from her soul.

One year and a day, one year and a day and she could erase this pain and pretend it had never happened. Asrian wasn't what she'd expected, but he also wasn't someone she'd have sought out to be mated to either. Nor did she plan on remaining with him a moment longer than she had to be, either.

Her mind rushed with the implications of what they'd done, and what it could mean as well. She knew her father wanted her to secure an heir, but what did Asrian want? What did she expect to get from this? There were so many questions and no answers to be found here, in the silence on the border of the Court of Nightmares. Not any foe she could from their court.

She misted, turning into shadows as she headed back to the palace, back to the people who had betrayed her.

Once inside, sodden and soaking wet, she ignored the curious glances of the men as she sloshed water everywhere. Lilith stopped in front of Asrian and Sinjinn and paused.

"I'll go to see these people, to see if they belong here or if it is an empty attempt to lure me into a false sense of your decency."

"Lilith…" Lara whispered sadly.

A Demon's Plaything

"You don't get to speak to me right now," Lilith uttered thickly through the emotion threatening to choke her.

"I'm still your sister!"

"You are, but you didn't trust me enough to tell me the truth either. You didn't trust me with your secrets while I poured mine out to you. I've never kept anything from you, including Court of Night secrets which I am now bound by law to report to my father. I told you, a princess of the Horde, our secrets which is punishable by death should he choose to enforce it. So no, you don't get to talk to me. I will retire for the night; in the morning, we can travel without worry of the Court of Nightmares attacking us."

"You don't have to tell him anything! They left you here with me, you chose this court. You're the heir of both, Lilith. You will rule both courts, and now you have a husband strong enough to rule them with you."

"I have a husband for one year and one day, and after that time I don't plan to ever see him again, or you, sister."

Lilith turned, lifting her soaked skirt to reveal her bare feet as she walked away from them with what little pride she had left. She'd barely made it to the hallway before a hand grabbed her, and she was pressed against the wall hard. Angry green eyes locked with hers as the giant heathen pinned her with his gaze.

"That was harsh, even for you. Are you sure you're not the Ice Queen, Lilith?" he snapped, his hands going flat beside her head, trapping her there. "Don't plan on seeing me after the handfasting time, hmm?" he continued icily.

"You think you have some say in what happens here, don't you? Newsflash, you don't. Once the time ends you'll vanish, but me? I'll be the soiled whore no one wants to touch after your hands leave their mark. The ill-fated queen who was sold to pay the tithe," she laughed soundlessly as she watched his face tighten with anger. "That is the truth of what we've agreed to. The Horde is feared, but the women they use, the ones they touch? They're considered trash, less even. You think you're my hero in my story, but you, you're the villain. So tell me, prince of the Horde, what do you expect to gain from this?"

"I haven't gotten that far yet. What I expected to find was a spoiled princess who complained entirely too much, which you're not, minus the complaining part. I expected to come here, to retrieve a bride and do what was needed. Instead, I get here and find the most beautiful creature that world has ever created, and she fucking hates me. Soiled whore? Never, you're perfect, innocent, and fire. So you can feel sorry for yourself if you want, but your sister? My sister, she had to hide from you because of that hate you're allowing to consume you. You sit in a fucking pile of ruins and stew on shit that you couldn't change, that we couldn't change. Have you considered what she felt, what she endured? You walked into the chaos, she survived it."

Lilith fought the tears as his words hit her. "Because of what she is, and all she had to do was tell me. Lying to me has put my life on the line, and not even you can question that law. She lied to me, my own sister who cried with me, who mourned the loss of our mother together. I told her everything, I trusted her enough to let her see my flaws, to know my weaknesses, and the entire time, she didn't trust me enough to tell me hers in return."

"And you can't get past that, or is it because she's what you hate most?"

"There's that too," she admitted as she ducked out of the cage his arms had created and started down the hallway.

"I'm not done talking," he snapped harshly.

"I'm freezing, so if you plan on finishing your little speech, you'll do it in the bedroom," she snapped back, her tone low as her teeth began to chatter as the cold in her bones mixed with the weariness and exhaustion she felt.

She dismissed him, only to scream in shock as she was lifted easily from the floor into his massive arms. She shrieked as his arms tightened and then the world rocked and spun around her as they appeared inside her bedroom. Her fingers bit into his flesh as the room continued to spin out of control around her. Lilith opened her mouth to speak but something soft and welcoming pushed against hers.

"Don't do that!" she hissed.

"Don't do what? Sift, or kiss you?" he laughed huskily. "I don't have to like you to fuck you, Lilith. You do respond so sweet to this fucking heathen king that it's hard to ignore or forget. Even if you do call me your heathen king, you enjoyed what we did last night, even if you regretted it afterwards."

"Well...work on it," she said as he gently set her down, ignoring the wide round eyes that stared up in shock at him. There was something hard that was very *hard* to miss as he'd set her down. She took a generous step away from him and let her eyes slowly lower to what had rubbed against her belly on the way down. "I'm...I should leave."

"It's your room," he noted huskily.

"Excuse me?" she uttered thickly as her eyes lifted to his, finally realizing she'd been staring at the obvious erection that his jeans did little to hide.

"It's your room," he said with a sexy grin lifting to play across his lips. The green in his eyes brightened, glowing as his hunger became evident. "You're trembling, little queen."

"I'm cold," she lied, because she was no longer trembling from the icy cold dress that clung to her like a second skin; no. Before her was a very virile, tough male who knew her with carnal knowledge and had apparently enjoyed what she had to offer him. "I should bathe."

"I'll join you, wife," he mused, his tongue slowly running over his full bottom lip as he watched the panic in her eyes spread. "Let me help you," he continued, snapping his fingers, and then she was naked in all her glory with a single thought of his mind.

The bathtub behind her hit her knees as she slowly backed up, and then she cried out as she fell into the warm water, heated by his magic as well as filled to the top. She spattered as she sat up, righting her body to glare up at him where he stood, sexual tension filling his endless emerald depths as he stared at her naked breasts.

Her hands came up to cover her nudity. A deep red blush ignited in her cheeks as she worried her bottom lip as her eyes closed against the lust she had seen banked in his gaze. She wanted to splash him with the heated water, to curse him to the gates if the underworld, and yet she did neither.

Her eyes peeked open as splashing sounded, and a stifled scream threatened to escape as she took in his cock at eye level. The thing was larger this close, and against her better judgment, she wanted to feel it, to test its weight in her hand. She hadn't been entirely naïve about sex, or what happened with a man and a woman, but neither had she expected to enjoy it. She'd heard enough grunts and screams of pain in her father's court to expect it to hurt, but that had quickly been replaced by pleasure.

"You keep looking at it like it's one of the Seven Wonders of the World and it won't ever go down, my little heathen queen."

"I'm not a heathen," she growled as she stared up into his heady gaze with anger boiling in her depths.

"You live in the ruins of a castle, you hunt meat for substance, and live like a lavish cavewoman. If that isn't a heathen queen to my heathen king, I don't know what is. Scoot your ass over unless you're planning to sit on my lap, which I'm not against. In fact, I'd rather you did with how hard that pretty stare of yours made my dick."

"You're crude and uncouth."

"And you're not? You rode my dick last night, so what does that make you, Lilith?"

"Desperate," she said. "Horrible, a traitor to my crown, and now because I actually liked it, ruined."

"And why would it make you ruined? Because you enjoyed sex? You're Fae; we fuck to feed, and because we enjoy it. There's nothing wrong with liking it. It makes you one of us."

"I'm lesser Fae; we do not feed by fucking. We need sustenance, and our status is defined by the character of the laws and rules we adhere to. You and your kind are ruled by emotions, by a need to fuck and destroy everything you touch. You are not the same as I am, and finding pleasure with you is against what the lesser caste will consider pure. If I'd hated it, hated you enough to make it a chore or a wifely duty, it would be different," she said thickly, her throat tightening with her words. "Instead, I found pleasure with you."

"And you don't want to?" he asked as he tipped his head as he sat in the tub, watching as she backed up as far as she could to keep from touching him.

"No, I wanted to hate it as much as I hate you."

"You don't hate me, you hate what I am. That's fine; most of the world hates the Horde. It comes with what we are, and what they construe us to be. Hell, my mother wasn't even from this world, and her people hate us too. We are the creatures of nightmares, the things that go bump in the night and legends you and your people use to keep your children in line. It doesn't mean we are what they say we are," he shrugged as he waved his hand and night bloom petals filled the tub, glowing as the floated above the surface.

"You and your people took my mother's corpse, hanging her on the gates of the Horde stronghold as a warning to the other castes of what happens lest they forget or be unable to pay the tithe. She hung there until I was sixteen, and her corpse became nothing but bones and eventually fell to the ground before your gates, forgotten. I took her then, brought her back home to bury. I don't even remember her or what she was like. I don't remember my people, or who they were before they became dust upon the floor of these ruins. Yet here, among the corpses and the dust, I stayed, away from court politics or drama. I could have gone home, could have brought Lara as a servant and given her a better life, but I wasn't willing to ask that of her. To ask her to pretend to be anything other than my sister seemed wrong. You want to know why I hate your kind. Because to me, you weren't legends that we used to keep our children in line, you played out every horror they'd ever whispered, proving it true to the children whose lives you ruined when you turned the Court of Shadows into a Court of Ruin and Ghosts that continue to haunt me."

"I didn't do this," he uttered as he ignored her stiffening as he pulled her closer, settling her astride on his lap. "The tithe has always come at the same time since the courts began to grow. If a court were unable to pay, the king would forfeit his life so that another in his line could secure it and their reign. It was like that before my father ever settled his murderous ass on his throne, and it was created by your people. We didn't make the rules of how much or how little was demanded. We didn't decide on the price that was paid for being unable to pay the tithe to the Horde. Your people did, and with it, they sealed their fate. I met your grandfather many times, and he was a warrior, Lilith. Proud, strong, and truthful. He fucked up, though; he told other courts to stand with him, and, to get out from beneath his thumb, they told my father what he planned, and sealed the fate of this court."

"That can't be true because who in their right mind

would try to take on the High Fae? That would be suicide."

He lifted a brow, staring at her as his mouth slowly lowered, kissing the hollow flesh just above her collarbone. "I'm starving, wife," he murmured before his hands captured her hips, lifting her until she was poised above his cock. "Will you feed me?" he asked, knowing she had no idea that her pain was calling to him, luring him into her mind as it rolled off of her in powerful waves.

Asrian's mother was a pain seeker, a demon who sought those suffering and fed until they were nothing more than a corpse. His Fae side had muted the call for death, instead allowing him to leave those he fed from alive. But Lilith, Lilith was a fucking buffet of endless food.

"I don't really have a choice, do I?" she whispered as she moaned, unable to contain it as his mouth continued to trail over the sensitive flesh.

"You do; you can choose to let me starve. You can deny what you want," he growled as her pussy rubbed against the hardened silk beneath the heated, fragrant water that was working against him like some aphrodisiac that was sending both of them to the point their need was painful. She rocked her hips, chewing her lip before she released it to stare him right in the eyes.

"I can choose? I choose to let you starve, heathen king," she hissed as she stood, ignoring the tightening of his hands on her hips. He snarled as he took her back down, pushing her beneath the water before his mouth crushed against hers beneath the floating petals.

A Demon's Plaything

Just as quickly as he'd done it, he disappeared. She rose from the water, peering around the room at the empty space. She rose, stepping from the tub into the silence of the room. Once dressed for bed, she sat on it, staring at the empty side. No matter what had happened, she hated losing Lara, and yet she felt her downstairs, bonding with her newfound family as surely as she felt her heart slowly cracking in fractured pieces. Walking away by choice was easier than knowing Lara would choose them and to be among them. And why wouldn't she? They could give her everything, and Lilith only had this place, this empty palace to offer her sister.

The candles in the room extinguished as she rested her head against the pillows, refusing to feel sorry for herself. Life had a way of knocking the ground out from beneath you, and she wasn't any different. Today, though, today had rocked her fucking foundation and left her trembling on unsteady ground. She felt as if she'd become lost in something the Court of Nightmares had attacked her with.

The door opened, and she sat up, watching as Asrian strolled in. He was dressed in nothing more than sweatpants that hugged his form snugly, doing little to hide the bulge that she'd only moments ago been touching her most intimate places with.

"I don't care if you plan to starve me, my sweet heathen queen, but I'm not leaving your bed. You don't have to touch me; hell, you don't have to want me here, but I'm here, and you're my wife. Most men wouldn't think twice about feeding elsewhere, but I'm not most men. So for a year, I'm yours, and you're mine, and we will be faithful to the vows we took before the Gods and Goddesses. So, you've been warned. If you touch another man, I will make your life hell, and his will end. You can promise me the same fate, but I doubt you'd care either way."

"Get in bed, I'm exhausted, and you're ruining my beauty sleep, Asrian."

"Not heathen king? That's progress."

"No, it's not heathen king, sleep."

"You got a smart little mouth, you know that, right?" he chuckled.

"So I've been told."

Chapter Ten

Lilith awoke being crushed to death. Something hot and heavy was crushing the air from her lungs as it pressed against her. She pushed at it, prying her tired eyes open to peer up over at the giant Fae who held her. She lifted her body, staring down at the giant brute that was larger than anything she'd ever imagined him to be. He looked peaceful, almost…normal in sleep. She silently took in the sinewy curves of his muscles, the ripple of washboard abs that bespoke of strength.

She inhaled the masculine scent he exuded. Before she could think better of it, she lowered her nose to his chest, inhaling of his unique scent. Her lips pressed against his flesh, slowly exploring the contour of it as her hair trailed over it. Lilith exhaled as a soft moan of desire escaped.

"You're molesting me in my sleep?" a sleepy tone filled the room, and Lilith lifted a guilty stare to the man she'd been exploring languidly, haphazardly against her better judgment. "No, no, continue. I'm here for your pleasure, wife. Take it in, it's all yours."

"I...I...fuck," she groaned as she lifted her body to her knees, staring down at his amused smirk as his sleepy eyes took in her oversized nightgown. "You were crushing me in your sleep."

"So you decided to sniff and molest me?" he shrugged as he rested his hands behind his head in a lazy, relaxed pose. "Sounds legit, I mean, when I'm being crushed, my response is to sniff my prey first, fight later. Having all the strategic information about my crusher is important," he mused.

"You're making fun of me?" she asked as she fought against the smile that tried to tip the corners of her lips. "Whatever, you smell...nice," she admitted. "Different than other males," her voice came out throaty, husky, and sounded like it belonged to someone else.

"You've spent a lot of time sniffing other men? No wonder you prefer to remain here, what would the rumors be if the queen went around sniffing everyone?" he chuckled.

She placed her red face into her hands and shook her head. "I've never sniffed anyone else before, nor have I woken up next to anyone other than my sister. I also tasted you, so there's that if you want to throw it at me." She dropped her hands and chuckled, staring at him as a smile played over her face and his went still, staring up at her as if something was wrong. "What?"

"You're fucking beautiful, but when you smile, you're fucking stunning," he admitted as he continued to look at her, his hand lifted, brushing over her cheek gently as he watched her smile fade.

"Thank you," she muttered, embarrassed at his

compliment. It was something she hadn't had many of since the Night Court was filled with blonde beauties with matching eyes and then there was her, darkness in a court of people who shone beautifully beneath the moon that fed them power.

"This is where you tell me how fucking handsome I am," he explained as her eyes rounded and she continued to stare at him.

"You're..." she stopped as she swallowed deeply and frowned.

"Wow, okay then. I know I'm not pretty like Cailean or Tor, but I didn't think I was that bad," he laughed.

"You're rough, which is different considering you're Fae. You smell like spices, mixed with fire and yet there's something else mixed into your genetics. But no, you're not displeasing to look at. In fact, I think I like looking at you, heathen king," she said, adding the last with a cheeky smile.

"Yeah? Wow, that's a high compliment from you," he laughed and then sifted. She stared at the spot he'd just been in and started to turn when he pushed her to the bed, claiming her mouth in a hard kiss that tore a deep moan from her lungs. Her nightgown vanished with his clothing, and she wrapped her legs around his waist, coming undone as his magical lips consumed her mind, as if he was literally sucking her will out through the kiss.

"Asrian," she whispered once his lips lifted from hers and he stared down at her, silently asking permission to continue.

A knock sounded at the door, and he growled as he turned his head, staring at it. She blushed as she waited, wondering who was outside the door and how they'd explain their current state of arousal should they enter to find them like this.

"Asrian, get it done already you slow-moving fuck," Tor shouted through the thick door. "We got things to do, and your wife's freshly plucked lady parts were not on our list today."

"Shut the fuck up you prick," Asrian snapped. His eyes heated as he slowly brought them back to Lilith's mortified face. "We'll be ready in a few minutes."

"You need help?" The awkwardness of the question hung in the air.

"No, Torin, I don't need help, nor does my wife," Asrian hissed beneath his breath as he lowered his mouth and kissed her forehead. "Pay him no heed, he's a heathen, like me. Get dressed, we can continue this later."

"I don't think that is wise, not unless you want a child," she said.

"I wouldn't mind kids; those little monsters tend to be a pleasant surprise. My brother and his wife, they have the triplets and those little ones, they're smart. They already sift, which is pretty unheard of at their age. But back to the point, I wouldn't be against a child if it happens, Lilith. And I'd be around to watch it grow. I'm not the type to ignore my responsibilities."

"One year and one day, so no kids," she grumbled as she left the bed, leaving him to stare after her as she moved to her chest of clothes. She had a few form-fitting dresses for traveling, ones she'd had made while at the Night Court, necessary items to thrive while alone in her own court.

"And if you're pregnant already?" he asked.

"Then we will handle it," she supplied crisply.

The idea of being pregnant was like ice water being dumped over her head. The knowledge that he'd expect to be in the child's life or participate was sobering. The Horde was notorious for spreading their seed wide and far, for breeding and leaving the poor mothers with mutated children who no caste accepted into their court behind.

No, she wouldn't be having any child anytime soon. She didn't want to be stuck with the Horde breathing down her neck if what he claimed was true. It was widely known that those triplets were the key to bringing the new Horde King to his knees, and as much as she desired it, she hated the idea of the poor wee things being used to achieve it.

"Get ready," he snapped sharply, his tone full of irritation. She closed her eyes against his heavy stare she could feel on her back. "We leave in ten minutes."

The door slammed behind him, and the heavy weight on her chest filled with the frustration and wariness she felt. It wasn't that she wanted to be so prickly, but it was hard to let go of the pain and fear, the unknowns and the consequences that being with him would leave on her. Cade hadn't responded when she had warned him what was coming, he hadn't even spoken before he'd walked away without looking back when she'd stopped to talk with him before rushing back to Lara.

Lilith had known what could happen if her father didn't work towards the tithe, and he hadn't. No matter what she told herself, her father was self-serving, self-indulged and uncaring who paid for his actions. His people starved at the gates to the court and instead of sharing what they had, he barred them from getting into the safety it would offer them.

She'd known the Horde would come, and when they did, they'd demand payment. Then rumors of the Summer Court being offered to give one daughter to a prince of the Horde had followed. Meaning there was an easy way out, which she knew her father would take if offered. His only focus was to keep his throne, and while he loved his children, he loved himself more. Yet she'd told herself he wouldn't do that to her. That turned out well.

So she'd warned Cade, and no matter how much she ignored the facts, he wouldn't be back after the year and one day; nor would anyone else. Men didn't want the women soiled by the Horde who they viewed in the lesser courts as ruined, tarnished things.

Ten minutes later, she was dressed, with weapons hanging from her hips and a silver bow with matching quiver and arrow tips hanging from her back. Her hair was braided into one thick, dark braid that was wrapped into a bun tied to her hair by jeweled pins.

The moment she entered the hall, silence met her. Asrian turned, taking in her dress and fine weapons before he started towards the doors. Outside, there were horses saddled and ready for them to use.

"We'll take them as far as the upper lands. Once there, we will need to sift into the Hidden Realm, where your people are," Sinjinn announced, obviously the one used to being in charge. "After that, we need to make a stop at the Guild before returning here."

"Guild?" Lara asked.

"It's where we will meet with the king and queen before returning here. We have to let them know the wedding has been consummated and that there were no hiccups with it."

"Define hiccup? I think I'm going to be a hiccup to him, and I'm not sure I'm ready to meet him and tell him I'm his sister," Lara admitted as she turned to Lilith, who had become as white as freshly fallen snow.

Lilith's heart lodged in her throat as she stared at Lara, and the idea of losing her struck her dumbfounded. This was happening; it wasn't just a nightmare, it was her new reality. She was losing the one person who had loved her unconditionally, without caring that she was a mishmash of two courts packaged into one.

"Let's get moving, shall we, ladies?" Cailean asked excitedly. He clapped his hands together, unaware of the tension between the sisters. His eyes slowly moved between them, and he frowned. His hand went to his tipped head as he scratched it. "Fairy fucks. Being Horde isn't so bad, *sis*."

Lilith expelled a shaky puff of air as she moved without thought, running from the hall to empty her stomach as the stark reality settled into her soul. Lara was Horde. She was the sister of the Horde King; sister to the monster who had sealed her fate with his generous offer. She had never felt so fucking alone in her entire life.

Chapter Eleven

The sun settled on the mountains, bathing the upper lands of Faery in its warming glow. Lilith hadn't spoken, hadn't said one single word since she'd thrown up repeatedly outside her great hall, right onto Asrian's boot-covered feet, much to her own horror.

Asrian spoke to his brothers in friendly banter, arguing over things she had no idea about. Lara rode beside her, answering for her when the men asked something. She laughed with them, told them of her version of the fight that had occurred so long ago, things she'd never told Lilith to date.

Everything felt as if it was happening to someone else. As if someone else was stuck in this horror of endless torment that continued to unravel her world thread by thread. She knew she should be thankful that they weren't of the same ilk their father had been, but things kept being brought to light, and every time it happened, it was something big, something that pushed her a little further over the edge.

She was on a horse, marching to meet people she'd thought long since perished, and the fucking Horde King. This wasn't happening. She'd dreamt of his death, relished the death blow she could never land, since the King of the Horde held a beast within him, one that couldn't be killed.

"We leave the horses here," Asrian said from beside her.

She turned, staring through him as the others began to dismount. She lifted her leg over, revealing her thigh as she dismounted and stood there awkwardly as she waited. She hated sifting; not the quickness, or ease of it, but the nausea and unsettled feeling when they landed. Not to mention, she had no idea where the Hidden Realm was and had never even heard of it before.

Lara stopped beside her as the men unharnessed and saddled the horses before slapping them on the rear, sending them away. The chilled air sent a few stray strands of Lilith's hair wafting through the air as they stood there, waiting to be sifted to the unknown.

"Breathe, Lilith," Lara uttered as she stared at her, her Fae eyes now tri-colored in turquoise and ice blue shades that were filled with endless galaxies within their depths. Her thick hair was darker, mixed colors of midnight and chocolate fighting for dominance as her brands pulsed. She looked away from her, hiding the traitorous tears that struggled to be let loose.

Lilith straightened her spine as Asrian reached for her, her flesh connecting with his sending a shock racing down her spine, zeroing in on her belly as heat pooled there. Stupid Fae and his stupid touch. He'd been silent since they'd left the palace, holding his tongue when she'd released her meager supper on his boots, and still, said nothing.

They sifted into a realm full of fragrant blooms and bubbling brooks, much like the one they'd just left. People milled about the small town they'd sifted to, hair as dark as the shadows that filled the world. Heart racing, Lilith smiled as those people turned, staring curiously at them as they slowly approached. Eyes; their eyes were filled with the dark galaxies she'd heard of, the beautiful darkness that filled the midnight skies and fed their powers as the night took control and shadows became abundant, adding to their power.

"I told you, not all of your court perished, and that's because my brothers and I got them out before he got to them," Sinjinn said beside her.

Lilith nodded silently in shock as she moved closer, listening to them playing in the streets in beautiful clothing, their current state more than most courts could afford for their people. They laughed with no fear for the Horde who approached them now.

"You're back so soon?" a woman's musical voice said from not far away, and Torin chuckled.

"I knew you'd be missing us, Liliana," he snorted, and a feminine shrill sounded, forcing Lilith to draw her blades as the familiar scream ripped through the air, but Lara was running towards the woman with her arms out.

"Mother!" she cried as she threw herself into the woman's astonished arms.

Lilith stifled a sob of disbelief as she watched the woman begin to cry, wiping away the tears that fell from

Lara's eyes. Her eyes, ice blue, rose to stare over Lara's head at Lilith, who stepped back, bumping into a hard form behind her. She swung around, staring at Asrian who was quickly doing the math of who held Lara.

This wasn't fucking happening.

"Lilith, oh, my baby!" the woman cried as she pulled Lara with her towards Lilith, who stood stone-still, unable to get words out. "Oh, look at you. You're so beautiful."

"You're dead! You're fucking dead," Lilith half hissed, half screamed as she forced Asrian to move away from her.

"No," she uttered. "I've been here."

Lilith slapped her, hard. "You left us. I waited for your rotting fucking corpse to fall from the Horde's castle walls so that we could bury you! You've been *here*? You abandoned us to come here? Who the fuck does that? Who abandons their children like that?"

"Lilith, I couldn't come back, not to find Lara dead. I thought her dead! I knew you'd be fine, you're your father's daughter, his heir, I couldn't come to get you. And I thought my sweet Lara had been among the dead, with her grandfather. So when they told me of our people who they'd saved, I came to them. They needed me with them. I am the Queen of Shadows, they needed me."

"I'm…I needed you! I have needed a mother, Lara needed a mother. When I found her, she was alone, filthy and alone. She had no idea how to hunt or how to survive, but then…" she paused, turning to stare at Lara. "She'd transitioned by then, hadn't you? How fucking pathetic I must have been," she whispered as the knowledge hit her. "That's why you disappeared at night when you thought I slept, to feed. And me, I spent countless hours securing food that I thought you needed. But you're High Fae, and I'm just *less*." She wiped at the tears that trailed down her cheeks. "Take me to the Night Court."

"You're my heir, too," Liliana said softly. "You don't have to go back there. I know it doesn't call to you, not as our own court must. The shadows crave you, daughter. I feel them."

"I renounce your throne," she hissed.

"You can't, you can't just renounce it. It needs an heir that can hold it. Without one, the Shadow Court cannot be within the ranks of the lesser courts, and the Horde needs them now more than ever. We're not the only ones who survived; I sent thousands into the woods, Lilith. War is coming, and I have to have an heir at my side."

"You have one, your daughter. I am not your heir anymore; I am Lilith, Heir to the Court of the Night, and I renounce your throne and your bloodline."

"It doesn't work like that, Lilith. Did your father teach you nothing?"

"My *father* couldn't stand to even look at me! He looked at me and saw you, so my entire life before I left him was lived inside a fucking room people weren't allowed into because I may have died and needed protection. My life was being sheltered because Gods forbid he lose his heir, or have to look at her face that reminded him of his ghosts. So teach me? No, strangers came into my room and taught me to rule, that in times of need or time of trickery an heir could walk away by renouncing her bloodline if those she chose to leave had used trickery upon her. I've been nothing but tricked by you and Lara. I've been lied to and abandoned. I love you both, but for my sanity, I renounce you both. Lara deserves to be your heir; she's strong enough to stand against anything, considering she's Horde Fae."

It wasn't selfish, she told herself. To keep Lara close, she'd renounced the line. To keep her sister with her, she'd renounced the line. She'd forced Lara to remain in the lower realm of Faery by doing so. She'd sealed the line, protected her people, and now Lara couldn't abandon her.

"Lilith, I wasn't going to ever leave you."

"Get out of my fucking head, Lara," she warned coldly.

"You're my heart. You're my sister by choice, let alone bloodline. I needed you, I need you so much. I don't need a title!"

"You do because holding them both is too much for one person. She needs an heir, you're her heir. I can't be the queen of both courts, and I'm going to kill him for using me to pay the tithe. Do you understand? I'm going to murder my father for using me to pay it when he didn't have to. I'm going to save myself from what telling you those secrets cost me before that betrayal costs me my life."

"He…didn't, you're…oh no," Liliana said as she surveyed the men around them. "I should have been there to gather it, to pay it for both courts."

"You weren't there to protect us." Lara's tone was angry, her hand absently stroking Lilith's arm to calm the anger and rage that burned through her sister's soul.

She'd paid for their deaths, for the people who now watched them. She'd poured every ounce of energy into rebuilding a court that the world didn't care about, and this entire time they'd been here or elsewhere while their heir worked from morning until night, righting the kingdom for them. All for the ghost she believed watched her, watched them. And here there were thousands of them, alive.

Lilith had paid the tithe selflessly, knowing her father could have paid it if he'd cared to, meanwhile allowing her other court to starve to death, slowly. She'd trotted into the Horde's stronghold and removed the corpse she'd thought belonged to her mother at the tender age of sixteen, bringing it home to be buried in a grave fit for a queen that she herself had erected. Endless days she'd begged her father to see her, until she'd stopped caring if he ever did. He'd taken lovers, producing children he bragged about, and yet his own heir was banned from his hall unless it was time for her presence to remind the court he had one.

Law stated that each caste of the lesser Fae have an heir for when the tithe came due, and he'd made sure they knew. He'd recited her duties, reminded her of what was to come, and then she'd been free to leave until he summoned her again. He hadn't cared that she rather remain in the ruins of a palace than locked in a room.

"What do *you* want, Lilith?" Asrian asked, and her ice blue eyes lifted to his. In her entire life, no one had ever asked her that.

"I don't want to be here."

He grabbed her, vanishing into thin air as Lara watched.

Chapter Twelve

They sifted right outside of the Guild, and he flinched as something sailed past his head. He moved, reaching for Lilith but she dodged the attack, turning to look at where it had come from. She reached behind her, unsheathing an arrow which she nocked and sent sailing at the demons that were on the edge of the warded barrier. One after another, she hit her target perfectly, skillfully. All the pent-up rage was being given to the demons as one after another fell to the volley of arrows she let loose.

"Gods, she's like Zelda, only prettier," a female voice said with a chuckle. Asrian flinched at the sound of Erie's voice and then felt his brethren as they sifted outside to see what or who had entered their barrier, pausing to take in the lone female slowly chiseling away at the demons who kept coming.

"Lilith, her name is Lilith, and she's my bride," he admitted.

"Does she like you, because her aim is pretty

outstanding, and if she doesn't, it's going to suck to be you, dude," she laughed as she clapped her hands and wiggled her eyebrows.

"Outstanding observation, Erie," he groaned. "Don't give her too many ideas, she may use them."

Lilith exhaled before letting an arrow sail through the night, hitting a demon right through the eye. Her head tilted as it didn't fall, and then she turned towards him and went still. Asrian followed her eyes, flinching as Ryder stood behind them, in his beast's form.

"This should be fun," he muttered.

Synthia sifted in beside Ryder, her gaze dropping to the arrow and then up into Lilith's terrified eyes. She expelled a soft sigh as she realized what the problem was.

"Fairy, you're freaking her out. Your father slaughtered her people, so change before I turn you into a frog or something clever. Welcome, Lilith. I'm Synthia, this is Ryder, and you need to lower the bow," she said as Lilith brought it up and aimed it right at Ryder.

"Fucking problem?" Zahruk asked as he made his way down the stairs and noted the tense situation. "You let that loose, sweetheart, you die."

"Lilith, it won't kill him." Asrian stepped in front of it. "It's been an intense few hours, I get it. It's not often you find out your sister and best friend was spawned from Alazander, or that your dead mother isn't even dead at all. But that arrow, it won't kill him. He isn't your enemy. He isn't the one you want to hurt."

"It won't kill him, but it won't be pleasant either."

"Wait, what did you say about Alazander, am I the

only one who heard it?" Synthia asked, but they ignored her even as the brothers around them gaped at what Asrian had said.

"Oh, I like her, she's got big balls!" Erie laughed, her red hair a mass of unruly curls as she nodded her head and pointed at Lilith. "She gets an invite to girl time this week! Right? Right. So glad you agree."

"Erie, this isn't the time," Synthia hissed as she stepped away from Ryder.

"Pet?" Ryder growled.

"Love you, but I have babies to tend to and all that, and I'm not sure I love you enough this week to take an arrow for you. Besides, she's right, it won't kill you."

One minute she held her bow, arrow at the ready, and the next she was standing there with her hands still in that position but nothing in them. She blinked, staring at the Horde King, who held it, his golden eyes alight with laughter.

"Welcome, Queen of Shadows and Night, to the Assassin's Guild. While I suspect you may not like me, you don't know me. Please wait to hate me until I give you an actual reason to. I can either be your friend, or I can destroy you and solve Asrian's problem of an unwanted bride. I don't enjoy your father or much care for any man who can toss his own daughter to the Horde so he doesn't have to get off his ass to collect twenty percent of the tithe I asked for."

"You asked for twenty percent?" Her heart dropped at his words.

"I asked for anything he could spare, you were what he offered."

"Because if you took me, he could blame you for

ruining the court and taking his heir," she assumed.

"Most likely, yes. He seemed all too willing to hand you over, but we don't intend to harm you. You will be placed on his throne with Asrian by your side. At that time, you can choose to remain with him as your absent husband, or remarry."

"What?" Asrian uttered. "No, I *am* her husband!"

Ryder lifted a brow in question in Asrian's direction and then shrugged. "You two work it out. I have too many courts to deal with as is."

"Yeah, about that. You remember the woman we spared, the one who was barely breathing who we were supposed to string from the walls of the Stronghold? She's the Queen of Shadows, and technically still is the Queen of the Night Court."

"Liliana is the Queen of the Night Court too?" he asked as he folded his arms, not releasing her bow.

"It's quite the tale."

"Your father raped my mother," Lilith said coldly. "My sister is your sister."

"The Horde has one female child, woman."

"Now it has two, beast."

"Watch your tongue." Ryder's growl reverberated from deep in his chest.

"Or what, you'll skin me alive, hang me from your walls? I might actually welcome it right now. And I don't really like you or your people. You take, you murder, and you rape women and leave monsters behind for us to deal with. Do you know what happens to a lesser Fae when the Horde comes through and uses them? When they leave their whelps behind? Or do you even care, because once they've been with the Horde, they're soiled garbage that is tossed aside. They're thrown out of the courts, no shelter and no food. If they can work, they may survive, but more often than not the Horde takes only the prettiest ones, which means they end up dead in the woods, or birth their bastards and trade them to be used as guard dogs, or worse for target practice. Lara was lucky she was spared. She was lucky I found her when I did because she may be Horde, but she is nothing like you, which wouldn't have changed what they would have done to her. She is everything right in the world, everything nice. So if you want to skin me, monster, let's dance. I'm done being pushed around and used."

"I love you too, sis," Lara said, causing Lilith's shoulders to droop.

"Is this your idea of not here? Because here is almost worse than there." Lilith muttered.

"Lilith, you're loved. You're wanted, even if your father couldn't admit that to you. He loved you once, more than life. More than his throne," Liliana whispered through the crowd.

"I don't need love, what I need is to be left alone."

"No, you don't. We can feel it, you know. Lara and I are both empath, we feel your needs. We feel the betrayal you think has been done to you. Pushing us away to protect the Court of Shadows isn't going to protect it from joining this war. We're in it already. We've trained, we're ready to defend Faery. You and your sister, however, will remain away from the battlefield during it."

"I've trained to kill him since the moment I could walk, woman!" she hissed.

"Ryder didn't rape me. He didn't slaughter our people. Ryder saved us, vowing that what happened to the dragons would never happen again. Without him, it would have been my corpse you retrieved outside the Horde stronghold that day. Without him intervening, our people would be nothing but a memory in a history book. I know it's hard to let it go, Lilith. I know you've spent your life planning to defend your people, but you have to. It's consuming you from within."

"Bouncing big balls," Erie chuckled.

"Is she normal?" Lara asked as she took in Erie. "She's related?" she asked Sinjinn, who chuckled at her response.

"She's somewhat adopted, I think. She comes here to rest when Callaghan is healing from Gods know what she's done to him. She's pretty much insane, but you learn to roll with it."

"My father took you, and you had her?" Ryder asked as his golden eyes seemed to see through Lara, unsettling Lilith, who stepped closer, ready to defend her.

"He won't hurt me. He's blood; I can feel it and so can he. Just as I felt the brothers when they appeared. I'm not leaving you, ever. You saved me, even if you don't think you did. I was preparing to kill myself when you showed up that day. I'd found enough iron to drink that it would have worked, but you strolled right in and smiled at me, and I knew everything was going to be okay. I am not as strong as you are, Lilith, not fit to rule."

"You're stronger than you think you are, and they're not your family. I am. I don't care what you feel, or

A Demon's Plaything

what they do. You belong with us, with your people."

"The demons are rallying; maybe we should take this inside and make some coffee?" Synthia offered.

"I sleep with Lilith," Asrian snapped.

"Well Fairy fucking Saints, Asrian, we sure hope so. Or you'd have some 'splaining to do, bro," Ristan smirked, his silver eyes slowly taking in the small female. "Damn, she's tiny. You mated with her and managed not to break her. I guess I can't call you *Wreck-It Ralph* anymore."

"Inside, before Lucifer shows back up searching for Lucian and Lena," Ryder grumbled. "He's been here five times this week. I'm about to sic Erie on him."

"Ooh, I like him. He's cheeky." She smirked.

"Inside."

Chapter Thirteen

Lilith stood to the far side of the room, away from the creatures who talked, uncaring that she listened. They seemed...normal, as if they did this a lot. Lara was laughing at something Synthia said, and then they both paused, turning those eyes on Lilith. She narrowed hers, uncaring if the Goddess liked her or not. She hadn't come here to make new friends or allies, and she just wanted to forget this day had ever happened.

Her mother was alive, alive and here. It felt like a betrayal, like she hadn't been worth coming back to. Her entire life had been lived with the knowledge that Liliana had sacrificed herself to the Horde, and with it, the raw, never-ending anger and need for revenge that had driven her. Now, now everything she'd ever believed was being twisted, and no matter how hard she struggled to accept it, it wouldn't sink in.

Lara would need a court. One strong enough to accept and protect her against the people who would try to disavow her for the blood she carried. The Court of Shadows would make any of the lesser courts pause, and by releasing her claim, relinquishing her birthright to claim it, she had both protected her sister while managing to ensure she stayed close. Lara's eyes settled on her once more, as if she felt what Lilith's inner battle was, and a sad frown displayed over her lips. Lara had always had an uncanny way of knowing Lilith's thoughts or moods, but an empath? She'd never even dreamt it possible since she'd believed her the child of a human male, and not a High Fae's bastard-born-child.

She watched as Lara moved closer, settling against the wall that Lilith leaned against, far from the Fae in the room. Her dark, multicolored hair caught the light and shimmered as she turned her tri-colored eyes on her. "I know you think it will protect me, but what about you? What about what you need? The Shadow Court is our home, Lilith. Ours. I'm still me, just different. You accepted me before I could explain, and the moment you vowed to murder any Horde you could find, I decided not to tell you what I was. I had been alone for so long, so scared that others would discover what I was and make it known to the world. But you, you walked in and smiled, and I knew I'd never be alone again, I just felt it. We're sisters, first and foremost, always. If you still want to relinquish the claim, I can't stop you. I can only ask that you not do it for me because you're stronger, smarter, and able to rule our people far better than I can or will ever be able to. Your father hurt you, and I know you mean to kill him—I think I knew it before you did. But he is your father, Lilith. You do love him, and right now the pain is speaking. Your anger is legendary but mixed with the pain you feel, you're a powerhouse, ready to explode," she said softly, her eyes moving to their mother, who watched them from across the room. "You should take some time to think about it first, and I think you should give her a chance to explain it from her perspective. Your father was obsessed with her; he'd never have let her go if he'd known she was alive. A queen is nothing without her people, and her world is her people. Her responsibility was the people of her kingdom first, and her family second."

"I don't need the semantics of ruling, Lara. I know why she did it, and I don't hate her for it, because I'd have done the same in her place. But all these years we've mourned her, we've spent countless hours building a shrine in her memory as we righted the debts owed in her name, and now here she is, alive and living carefree without hardship. What about what we endured to right the court? To mend the path to bring it back? My entire life has been spent plotting to avenge her, and here she is, unharmed and alive. I don't know what to do now, how to move forward. I don't have a purpose anymore."

"You're the heir to two of the most powerful courts in the lower realm, Lilith. You're a leader to the people of the night; you feed them while your father spends his hours in lavish accommodations. You are the chosen heir, not by birth, but for the love you give your people. That is something no one can take away from you. And you have him at your side now," she said as she nodded to where Asrian was walking towards them. "Use him, strike fear into those who threaten the Night Court, and make your claim felt. They intend to remove your father from his throne, which means you will be the Queen of the Night Court. Rule, fix the breach between the court and the people, and make it the place you want it to be. Feed the hungry, care for the weak, because that is who you are."

As he paused on front of her, Asrian asked, "Are you hungry or tired?"

"A little of both, but mostly the latter of the two," she admitted.

"Our room is ready if you are, Lilith."

She blushed as the room grew silent. Lilith peered at the others before letting Asrian direct her in the opposite direction, towards a staircase that led to a different section of the Guild. A few more stairways and several minutes later, they entered what appeared to be a sitting area, one that had several hallways which all led in different directions.

"We're down here," he said, slipping his much larger hand around her tiny one. His hand dwarfed hers, engulfing it and yet it was gentle. The touch sent shocks of awareness awakening through her until her heartbeat increased, and her legs waited to stop in place as she reacted to him, to his touch. "Today was a lot to take in."

"I didn't handle it well," she admitted. She'd been horrified, and her entire world had been ripped out from beneath her feet, and she'd panicked, rejecting everything. "I've spent my entire life believing she was dead, and this entire time, she's been living in luxury while our people suffered. And Lara, she needed her the most. You have no idea what being Horde means in our world. It's a stigma most people hate; people fear them and react based on that alone."

"But not you?" he asked slyly.

"I loathe the Horde, yes, but not her, not the unwanted castaways they abuse. They're blameless victims, born of violence on most occasions. I can admit that not all are as bad as we've been told, or violent."

Asrian hadn't been; in fact, he'd been gentle with her. He'd done what no one else in her life had ever done. He'd asked her what she wanted, and he'd meant it. Asrian hadn't needed to care what she'd wanted, but he had. He'd sensed her need.

"So I'm not that bad, huh?" he chuckled, and she pulled on his hand, forcing him to stop and look at her.

"Today when you asked me what I wanted, it was the first time anyone has ever asked me that question. It was the first time anyone cared to. Lara has always loved me, that I do not doubt, but I am the one who took care of her. Thank you," she uttered awkwardly. "And no, I don't think you're so bad. But you're Horde, heathen king. Actually, since I am no longer queen, you're just a heathen prince now."

"Titles don't make my dick hard, Lilith. You do, though."

"That's…sweet, almost. I think. You do know you're rather crude, right?" When he just smiled, she rolled her eyes skyward and let him continue moving them down the hall.

"I'm not good with words or beating around the bush. I say what I mean, and I mean what I say. You were supposed to be an easy thing to hit and quit, but I have this feeling you won't be. People suck, I won't argue that. But the Horde isn't all monsters and mayhem. We have good ones too, and we have some baddies. But we're trying to fix it. We've been trying for a long time, even before we killed our father. You want to know how he saved her. We got there before he did that day when it went down. Ryder told her everything that was coming, and what to do. He explained it to her, and she knew her own court would pay for what they'd done against the Horde. She helped us get people out, but before we could get Lara out—which by the way, we had no fucking clue she was related to us—without suspicion arising, my father struck the Court of Night. She raced to it to protect *you*. You and your sister were her entire world, but we couldn't stop him from attacking it, and she offered herself up to pay the tithe, but he wasn't exactly lenient enough to take her and be done.

"He beat her; Alazander beat her so fucking badly that we weren't sure she'd survive it. So Ryder took her to where her people had been hidden and left her. We ruined a corpse, making sure our father would never know the difference between it and what he'd done to your mother, and we hung it from the wall. See, the thing is, we didn't put it together, or why she'd run to the Night Court until now; we didn't know you were hers, or we could have righted the wrong. You think it was easy for her to decide to stay with her people instead of you? It wasn't. She argued it over and over again, but if she'd returned, she'd have been hunted by the hounds and dragged back to him, my father. By the time Ryder killed our father, so many years had passed, and there had been no sight or word of Lara surviving the attacks—and you, she knew you were alive and well. So put yourself in her shoes, see it through a queen's eyes. Her people needed her, and you didn't. She sent people out of that realm, I'm guessing to check on you. I'm also guessing they returned and told her you were a fucking warrior who was surviving."

"I understand her choices. I know why she did it, but once he was dead, once the threat had passed, she should have brought the people back."

"Go back to what? A pile of ruins, debt to the other courts who want the Court of Shadows destroyed? She had always planned to come back, but on top of everything happening, and everything that has happened, Faery itself is now in peril."

"If I feed you, will you shut up?" she asked, glancing at him sideways.

"So to get you into bed, all I have to do is talk? Why didn't you just start with that?" he chuckled as he picked her up without warning, rushing down the hallway.

"Put me down, giant oaf! You'll break me if you drop me from here," she shrieked as she held onto him tightly, her arms going around his throat tightly as she held onto him for dear life.

"You're afraid of heights?" he laughed.

"No, I'm not afraid of anything," she lied, her eyes dropping from where his mouth was entirely too close to hers. His breath fanned her flesh, and before she could stop it, her tongue came out to lick her own in anticipation.

"You're so fucked," he muttered as his eyes followed her tongue with heat banking in their emerald depths.

Chapter Fourteen

The bedroom was lavish, done in soft green and cream colors. Lilith swallowed hard as she took in the large bed, but a glance at Asrian's hulking frame confirmed the need. The covers had been pulled back, and pillows were scattered aside already, as if someone had anticipated them needing rest.

"I had food brought up for you," he said as he scratched the back of his neck, staring at the bed. "After you're fed, you can either feed me or not. I won't ask it of you tonight. I'm an asshole, but not that big of one. The choice is yours," he grumbled as he placed a tray of fruit, meat, and cheese onto a small table that sat in the corner. "I didn't know what you wanted or liked, so I just grabbed a little of everything."

"It's great, really," she said as she moved closer, taking in the spread of food. She picked up a red thing, staring at it before plopping it between her lips as he watched her with wide eyes.

"I forgot you have not been outside of Faery, but

that was a strawberry," he chuckled as she plucked the leaves from between her now red lips. "You don't eat that part, you take it off," he explained before removing the leaves from the next. "Like this," he continued before holding it to her lips, watching as she opened them to accept his offering. Her lips clamped around his finger as she took it, sucking the juice from his digit. "Gods, woman," he uttered as he watched her licking the juice from her lips.

"Did I do it wrong?" she frowned, and he smirked, his eyes alight with laughter. "I have never tasted anything like it. It's…different." She picked up a cherry and plucked the stem from it, biting into it. "Ouch," she said around a mouthful of fruit. She pulled the pit out and eyed it before looking around for a trash bin. "These are not right."

"You're supposed to suck the fruit from the pit," he said, covering his mouth as she watched him. He observed her as she picked up a banana. "Here, like so," he grabbed for it, taking it before she could bite into it with the peel still on. He handed it back to her and watched as those sweet red lips wrapped around it. "I think you should eat the meat, it might be safer for my sanity."

She smirked, watching his eyes as she took more of the banana between her lips. She chewed it as his eyes burned with heat. "It's good. I like my mouth full," she shrugged, and his lips opened and closed before he shook his head.

"That's naughty," he muttered as he stepped closer, pulling her body against his. She was tiny compared to him, almost childlike in structure and full hot-blooded woman, with sass to her that he rather enjoyed. He wrapped his hands around her thin waist. "I'd like your mouth full too."

"I'm not sure that would be safe," she said lifting her face to stare up at him. "I see food but no wine?"

"I didn't think after today you'd want to stay up long enough to indulge in it," he shrugged as he nodded towards a cupboard. "To get it, I'd have to let you go, and I really don't fucking want to yet," he admitted as he lowered his mouth to hers, gently nudging her lips apart as he captured her tongue in a dance of chaotic need. His hand slowly snaked up her back, pulling her hair back hard as he claimed her mouth. The moan that escaped them both filled the room as he lifted her, allowing her legs to wrap around his waist as he released her hair, moving them towards the cupboard. Small hands splayed on his neck, holding him to her as her body pressed against his hard muscles.

He set her on the counter, lifting the skirt of her dress to expose her thighs, which he squeezed as he pulled his mouth away from hers begrudgingly. He reached above her head and brought down two glasses, setting them beside her before he kicked open the cooler, bending to grab the wine. She bent down with him, grabbing the hem of his shirt, pulling it up as he rose to stand. Hesitantly, she tried to lift it up over his head but failed. He set the bottle down and pulled the shirt off, tossing it to the floor.

Lilith's shaking fingers touched the hard, sinewy muscles that begged to be touched, kissed. She bent her head, trailing her fingers over his abs before her tongue followed the same path. His fingers brushed her hair, pushing it from her face as he watched her. His body straightened, and then he brought her mouth up to his, forgetting the wine as he kissed her drunk with just his mouth.

His hands moved between them, lifting her as he reached for the thin wisp of material that barred him from what was his. He pulled his mouth away, resting his forehead against hers as she gasped for air, pulling it deep into her lungs.

"I won't be able to stop in a moment, so decide," he demanded huskily as she pulled back, placing her hand against his cheek, cupping it as she wiggled her pussy against his knuckles, which were grazing her flesh. "If we do this, you're mine. I won't give you up. Not now, not in a fucking year. Do you understand me, Lilith? I don't crave women, nor have I ever slept with one more than once. Ever. You, I fucking crave you, and it drives me insane. Your flesh, your taste, the shadows that escape when you find your release," he growled thickly.

"Fine, just make this ache stop, Asrian. Now," she snarled as she reached for his hair, pulling his mouth flush against hers with urgency. "Make me feel you."

Her clothes vanished with his, and before she could register what he'd done, he lifted her up and pushed into the sheath of her body, filling her until she cried out with the fullness of him. His hands used her hips, lifting and settling her until she was coming unraveled, murmuring his name as passion took precedence, and desire consumed her.

She was so fucking tight, her body clenching against his again and again until he growled from the constant feeling of her. He walked with her to the bed, lifting her and tossing her down to bounce on the mattress as the orgasm continued to rock through her. Asrian knelt in front of her, lifting her up to position her on her arms and knees as he nudged her legs apart.

The moment he pushed inside, she bucked against him. He felt every fucking inch of her as he filled her body, marking her as his as his brands began to swirl. Her own pulsed, subtle as the shadows that clung to her enveloped parts of her in a sort of mist of darkness that seeped from within her. She murmured his name over and over, begging him for more as his body slammed into her tight pussy. She was delicate and yet she was wild with need. He didn't care that she'd be marked come sunrise, because neither did she as she slammed backwards, taking all he had to give until her body trembled and her head lifted, screams of pleasure filling the room.

"Gods," he snapped as she sent him over the edge taking her with him as her body clenched and milked his, leaving him trembling from the force of his own release. "You're so mine," he uttered as he turned on his side, not removing his cock from her body before he lifted her leg, slowly working her clit as he prepared for round two. "I'm going to make you sore, so fucking sore that every time you flinch tomorrow, I'll know you are thinking of me and remembering tonight."

"You can try, heathen, but I find I enjoy this part of being married to you."

"Is that a challenge?"

"Did it work to goad you into more?" she asked huskily.

"Fuck yes," he chuckled.

"Then yes, it was."

Chapter Fifteen

It was three days before they emerged from the bedroom, and no one dared interrupt them either. Time passed and yet held no meaning as they learned one another, discovering things the other had never told anyone else. On the third day, her mother knocked, and she knew her time of avoiding her while learning how to pleasure and understand this man she'd found herself tied to for an entire year could only work for so long.

"She isn't going to keep going away for much longer," Asrian muttered as he absently stroked her hip. He leaned over, trailing his lips over the curve of it and down thigh before he lifted his hand and brought it down hard on her ass.

"Ouch!" she growled before she rolled them until she straddled him, staring down with a wide grin. "She will hear us."

"I don't think there's anyone in this place who didn't hear us, Lilith. In fact, they may be singing my praise back in Faery with the portals open; they probably have heard you screaming about how fantastic my cock was there too."

"I wasn't that loud."

"Um, okay. If that's what you want to go with. Remember, I tried to leave the bed twice, and you kept begging me for more."

"Is that how we're playing this?" she laughed as she pushed her flesh against his cock. "You are the one who keeps getting hard."

"That's never been an issue," he laughed as he watched her, her pain slowly escaping as she tried to ignore it, but failed. He'd fed from it gluttonously as she'd hidden in the room with him. She'd known he fed from her, and she hadn't cared. Instead, she'd let him take the pain from her. Not many cared for demons or even half demons taking from them, and she'd watched him feed with a mixture of wonder. Lilith had openly watched him, curious to see and feel what happened when he did it. Then the little minx did the last thing he'd expected: she'd pushed more of her emotions into the bond, giving it to him. "We're being summoned," he grumbled as he rolled them and pushed into her body. Her scream was captured by his mouth, and his throaty laughter was addicting. "The king wishes us to get the fuck out of bed and get downstairs so your mother stops pacing and calling me a fucking heathen."

"She really is my mother," she laughed. "Tell the king we will be down when we're done fucking. Unless he wants us down there, like this," she purred.

"I'd rather not see you like this," Ryder grumbled from the far corner of the room, where he faced the wall. Asrian chuckled and pulled the covers over them, staring down at her. "Your mother is very…impatient to assure Asrian didn't kill you, or worse," he muttered gruffly.

"Tell her I'm coming," she said.

"Apparently, we're all very aware of that fact," he said with a straight face. "There's also the fact that we've been made aware of an assassination attempt on the King of the Night Court. He's been gravely wounded and has called his heir home. We travel to the Night Court within the hour, be ready."

"Wait, *we?* As in you're coming with us?"

"The Horde has managed and protected the lower caste since the pact went into effect. An attempt on his life in his own court is against the laws, and I will have no choice but to reinforce them. The tithe is due because of the pact, and I will uphold my end of it. Especially considering who you lay beneath, and the fact that something cannot be undone," he pointed out with a sad look. "I will not have them denying your claim on the throne now that you are as you say, soiled. They may have signed the pact, but they forgot my end of the arrangement."

"Which was?" she asked carefully.

"Horde children were to be brought to us, to live freely without being harmed or mistreated. If what you say is true, and I assume it is with your willingness to hand your birthright over to Lara, then they need to be reminded of the deal. If they choose to ignore it afterwards, they can grace my dungeons and become my vellum. I find I'm short of it since abolishing the law and freeing those creatures my father kept to harvest flesh to create it from."

"That was true? Your father signed his laws with the vellum created from the flesh of his enemies?" She swallowed hard.

"Whatever you heard of him, he did worse. A lot worse, which I cannot even begin to atone for, nor will I try. What I will and can do is be better than he was. I can be just and lead the Horde through strength. That is the only promise I can make you, Lilith. It is the same one I have made to your mother. I do not accept you rescinding your court. Later, when your mother is tired of ruling, we will revisit it. I assure you, as my sister and yours, she will be more than fucking protected. She will be loved by all of us and accepted, and those who don't can leave Faery as a whole or die there. That choice will be given to them by me and her brethren."

"You'd do that for her?" she queried.

"Absolutely, and any other bastard-born children my father sired, which I am sure is many. He wasn't kind, and I'm sure as we move deeper into repairing the damages, we'll discover many other children he sired and abandoned. But this is now, not the past. Whatever happened back then, it was then, and we are not there anymore. We are the future, and we decide what happens now."

"And my child, if we create one and I decide not to remain with him past one year and a day as I have vowed?" Her words were hesitant, partly because her mind wasn't made up yet. She was unsure what she wanted, and while she enjoyed being with Asrian as they had been, she wasn't one hundred percent sure she wanted more from him. Not to mention, her child would be unable to ascend to her throne if he left, or if the Horde didn't back them with their strength.

"Lilith?" Asrian growled.

"I don't know what the future holds, but if we are to create a child, I need to know it is protected from those who wouldn't accept him as king."

"They'll accept him, or they will die," he sneered.

"I will make him king, and any who don't respect it will be the given the same option I already listed." Ryder's tone carried finality, the confidence of the king backing his own words. "Now, get dressed; we waste time, and your father has to decree you his heir before he leaves this plane for the next. I don't want to have to rack fucking heads together to make my point."

Ryder vanished from the room, and Asrian sat up, naked still. He turned his angry glare towards her, hurt mirroring in them. "Get dressed," he ordered, not bothering to use his glamour to assist her.

"You're angry?" she demanded as she stood naked, uncaring of the welts and bruises his hands had created over the time they'd shared in bed.

"You're damn right I'm fucking angry! I told you three days ago, if we do this, you're mine. Yet the first fucking chance you get, you plan to leave me. You ask my brother to accept our son should we have one because why, Lilith? Because you don't want my child sitting on your throne? He wouldn't be good enough for you? You've met us, you've met the king, and yet you're so fucking stuck in your ways and your beliefs that we're nothing but monsters that you'd throw any child we had away at the first chance!"

"That isn't what…"

"Get dressed!" he shouted, slamming the door closed in her face as he stormed out of the room, his hurt and anger flooding it until pain shot through her, as if he was feeding her every ounce of pain back he'd stolen all at once.

Her knees hit the floor, and she sat there, uncertain what the hell was happening as her heart raced and she felt nauseated. Tears burned her eyes, blurring her vision. A soft sob escaped her lips before she squelched it with the back of her hand. What the hell was wrong with her? Why had his anger and rejection felt like she was dying? She struggled back up to her feet, holding her chest as it tightened.

With effort, she dressed and slowly exited the room with one last glance at the crumpled sheets, leaving whatever had been forming between them in the room. She made it into the hallways before Synthia was there; the Queen of the Horde took one look at Lilith and her smile vanished.

"Oh, sweet baby Jesus," she muttered as she took in the crumpled riding dress and mussed hair. A breeze of soothing air brushed over Lilith, and she paused, looking down at the dress that was black and silky, a wealth of material that seemed as if it had been plucked from the shadows to create a masterpiece. Her hair was twisted and turned, and then a few loose curls were hanging from a braid that sat tight, yet comfortable on her head. "Much better," she muttered to herself before smiling, and the heavy weight of weapons were felt on her back and sides. "Do try not to stab or shoot my husband with them, I'm very partial to him. He doesn't get to get off that easy, not after giving me three babes at once."

"Okay," Lilith agreed as she stared at the Queen of the Horde, who looked almost human in her features. "Rumor has it you tried to kill him a few times?"

"Lilith, first rule about me is I don't try to do anything. I just do it."

"And the throat you ripped out?"

"Tasted like shit, but it drove the point home," she shrugged.

"It's not easy to forget the past."

"No, it's not supposed to be either. You lived it, but you survived. You're stronger for it, are you not?"

"I am."

"Then stop worrying about the past and look to the future. I understand your court was hit the hardest, but that wasn't by the king who now holds the Horde. Just as you are not responsible for what your people have suffered under your father's rule. That is why there are rules to the hierarchy. It's why there are heirs in place in the lesser Fae courts, isn't it?"

"It is."

"Then why do you blame him?"

"He was there," Lilith pointed out. "They were all there."

"They didn't want to be there, and from what I have heard, they were busy getting people out and risking their own lives to do so. I've watched him suffer endlessly for what his monster of a father ordered him to do. They're all fucked up for it, and yet that is the way of the Horde. They are the strongest caste in the entire world of Faery not because they played by the rules, but because they created them. They've worked tirelessly alone to save Faery. Everyone else pretended it wasn't dying, and yet these men fought to cure and fix it. That should speak of their character alone. You don't know them yet, but you will, Lilith. You're our family now, you are one of us."

"I don't think I will be past the year and day, Queen of the Horde."

"My name is Synthia, Goddess of the Fae. Meaning, all of the Fae, Lilith, even the lesser courts. I'm guessing you two had a fight, but what I have heard for the past few days wasn't fighting. It was the beginning of something good, something pure. Find it again."

"We're ready to ride, Syn," a tall blonde said as he strode to stand beside them.

"Thank you, Lachlan," she acknowledged.

"No problem, I came to peek at the dame who has Asrian in a rage. Pretty sure he just destroyed a few demons outside because of it."

"A few? Must not be that angry."

"Thousand. A few thousand demons which have been gathering out front of here for a couple of days. Erie is out being his cheerleader, although I'm pretty sure he didn't notice her. She is pretty, isn't she?" he murmured as he reached out and touched one of the black curls that trailed down her back. "Exquisite, really. And here father seemed so put out when they offered their daughters to pay the tithe. Idiot, his loss," he said absently.

"Don't worry, we chose a bride for you as well, Lachlan."

"I've been warned," he chuckled. His tri-colored eyes reminded her of the seas as he watched her. "I'm almost intrigued to meet mine. Almost, but not enough to do so," he smirked as he let his hand drop and turned to smile at Synthia. "I'll be outside to escort you to Ryder when you're ready."

"He doesn't address you as his queen?"

"No, we're not formal here, not unless we're in front of the courts. Sometimes even then we're not. It's our court; we tend to run it like we want to."

Lilith stared at Synthia's back as they headed down the hallway. She thought of what Asrian said, and what she thought. It hadn't been that she wouldn't want her son or theirs to be king; the people wouldn't, and she had needed to hear his brother say he'd protect them. She'd needed to know her child and his claim would be backed and that he'd be safe.

"Tell him that, exactly that," Synthia said with a backwards glance.

"Holy shit, you can read minds?" Lilith gasped.

Synthia shrugged and then nodded. "Sometimes, sometimes not," she explained. "I'm new to this Goddess thing, but some of the things happening are handy. Some are rather a nuisance."

"Noted."

Chapter Sixteen

They entered the Night Court just as the moon reached its precipice. Lilith stopped outside the gates, nodding to the guards before she tipped her head up and stared at the stars that burned brightly, as if they sensed that the Night Court needed their welcoming light.

Asrian had ignored her for the entire trek to the upper lands, and then Lachlan, one of his brothers she'd learned, had sifted her the rest of the way here. He hadn't said one word, not even looked in her direction that she'd noticed.

"You've come with them?" one of the guards whispered in a hiss loud enough that the others caught the same hesitancy, fear, and loathing that dripped from his tone.

"Yes, Lain, I have come with *them*, now open the gates and let us in. It was not a request," she hissed back, squaring her shoulders and staring him directly in the eye. Here she wasn't Lilith; she was Heir to the

Night and Queen of the Shadow Court. Here, she was the cold creature she'd been bred to be. "Unless you'd like to see what your heart looks like outside your body, open the fucking gate. I will not ask again."

"As you wish, Shadow Queen," he replied, peering over her head at where the Horde stood, waiting.

They walked into the central courtyard, fearful murmurs following them as they passed through, entering the main entrance as one large group. Liliana was covered in lace, her face hidden from those who would remember it. The inside of the castle was filled with the court's council and her sisters, all who stood as she entered, staring at her with something cold in their eyes. She was heir by right, but any of her sisters could challenge it if they dared. Luckily, they'd preferred to spend their days being pampered and tended to rather than wielding blades or training.

"Clear the room, leave the council, and one of the bloodline may remain. Summon the head of the guard and any officials who are not present," she announced as she headed towards the bed that sat in the middle of the room, candles burning around it as the death rattle sounded from her father's lungs.

She didn't falter as she approached, showing no fear even though the knowledge that he was dying hurt deeply. Lilith hadn't expected it to hurt, not this much. He was a selfish bastard, but he was her father. Leonidas had kept the court running; he'd fought off the other courts' sad attempts to take it by force, even though none had come close to succeeding. He'd sucked at being a father. But then, other factors played into it and everything else that had forged her life into what it was.

Once the guards had entered, she stood beside the bed where her father lay, dying.

"Who was protecting him?" she asked, watching the guards who stared back at her, eyes hard and filled with hatred. "I asked you a question. This is where you answer me."

"We don't answer to you. He's chosen a new heir, as you are soiled now."

Lilith turned to the council member who had spoken. She smiled. "Then bring her out, and I will challenge her now."

"That law is outdated," he snapped.

"Please, tell me how he made it known that he'd chosen a new heir."

"He told us," he lied.

"His throat is punctured by an iron blade, so how was he able to speak to tell you such a thing?"

"I am the heir now, Lilith. You've betrayed us," Hannah said firmly as she plucked an invisible piece of lint from her skirt, unable to make eye contact. "Therefore, I am the new Queen of the Night Court."

"Who was protecting our father, Hannah?" she asked again.

"I was, but the assassin was from your court, Queen of Shadows. Everyone knows shadows cannot be stopped."

"I have no court left, everyone knows that," Lilith laughed. She eyed the guard and where his hand went, to the iron blade that he wielded. Lilith could smell the blood on it; her bloodline's blood had been drawn with it. "You are aware of the powers that the Court of Night's bloodline wields, are you not?"

"You can control minds, wield the moon's power, and are stronger and faster than every court except the Court of Shadows."

"You forget, we can smell when our blood has been drawn by a certain weapon or enemy. My father's blood is on your blade, William." She didn't wait for him to respond. Instead, she turned into shadows and entered the three armed guards at once, splitting them apart from the inside as her shadows ripped and tore them to pieces. Screams erupted; blood sprayed and splattered the walls around Lilith as she solidified. "Anyone else help dethrone my father while I was out?"

"You can't do this! I am the chosen heir!" Hannah said as she stomped her foot and pumped her fist down at her side.

"You traitorous bitch," Lilith said in a deadly hiss before she sent her shadows to wrap around her sister's throat. Slowly, very slowly the air left her throat. Blood exploded from her lips, and her eyes went wide with horror before going limp. "An attack against the king is treason, so if any of you helped, you'll get this offer only once. Leave; stay and betray me and you will die."

"You're soiled! Even soiled he wouldn't agree that you weren't fit to be our queen!" Claudette, an elder Fae who looked as if she was at least a few thousand years old, screamed. "They killed our queen! They killed an entire court, and in their wake, they left their little bastards scattered all over the lower lands. You are not fit to be queen now, not with their taint on you or already growing within your womb." She cried out as her head tilted at an odd angle. Lilith smiled hauntingly as the woman's corpse crashed to the floor.

A Demon's Plaything

"I am not soiled, and they did not murder my mother."

"I watched it happen with my own eyes!" Lariat growled but didn't step forward.

"Oh, Lariat," my mother crooned as she lifted the lace veil. "You always were sweet, but they didn't kill me, they actually saved me. Had it not been for them, Alazander would have murdered me, and yet my beloved king wouldn't intervene or even beg for me, but you did."

Her hand touched his scarred face with a gentleness that was unsettling. They were familiar in a way that made Lilith give her mother some serious side-eye. Now was not the time for that shit. People gasped and rushed forward.

"Our queen is back! We are saved!"

A hand touched Lilith, and she looked down at her father, who was staring with wide eyes at her mother. His eyes moved between them, and then he pulled on her until she lowered next to him.

"Mmm..." he struggled to get the words out past the damage of his throat. Synthia moved closer and his eyes rounded as he took in the glow that resonated from her. Her hand touched mine and then his, and he was there, in her head.

"Mother...?"

"Is alive," she said out loud.

"You're my heir, my daughter. You're my soul, Lilith. The best of me," he said gently in her head. His eyes went wide as the tears filled Lilith's eyes, which she wiped away before anyone else could see the weakness. "You can hear me."

"I can hear you, father," she admitted, her eyes lowering to hold his. "Synthia is the Goddess of the Fae, the Horde King's wife."

"I need you to know I'm sorry. I'm sorry my grief consumed me. I'm so sorry I couldn't look at you without seeing her and hurting. I should have been better, more present. Instead, I pretended the court had remained the same, holding parties and locking out those who needed us. You'll have to fix it back to what it was, the glorious Night Court. The beauty it held; you can do that because you hold enough that the moon Goddess will bless you."

"I'm sorry you failed too because I needed you. I needed my parents, and instead of losing just one on that day, I lost you both. It's in the past, though, and I forgive you. I forgive you both," she said loud enough for her mother to hear.

She stepped back as her mother stepped closer, staring down into her husband's eyes. "I relinquish the Night Court or any hold I held on it. I give it to the daughter we created, your heir. I don't forgive you for neglecting her or locking her in a room. She was your heir, the moon in your sky and stronger than you could ever hope to be. You knew being of two courts would be hard on her, and yet she has yet to be trained to use your court's power. Did you see how she killed, how she defended *you*? She murdered your attackers using my power, not yours. You failed her, and you will die knowing that. The Goddess will not forgive you easily for failing her. I forgive you for what you did to me, and what you did in your grief, but allowing our daughter to travel to the Horde Kingdom to retrieve what she thought was my corpse? Never. She was only a child,

Leonidas! Our child, born of a love brighter than the moon and stars you so adore, and yet she traveled alone, unprotected through her enemies' courts to the High Fae lands; that is something not even the strongest of your warriors could have done."

He blinked as Lilith watched, his shoulders trembling with unshed tears he refused to let drop. She wanted to defend him, but her mother wasn't wrong. Plus, unless she wanted to openly support her father and challenge her mother and her words, she'd have to bite her tongue. She hated politics already.

"Enough," she announced. "I will rise to Queen tonight since the king is unable to rule any longer. Prepare the ceremony and open the gates to the kingdom."

"The people are upset, starving! They could loot or worse, there must be precautions taken," a member of the council said.

"I said open the gates; they're starving because you failed to speak your mind on the matter. You wanted to feed them, to bring them into the safety of the court, yet you said nothing. So we will let them in and feed them. Have the kitchen prepare a feast, quickly. Something easy, and enough to feed an entire caste of Fae," she continued.

"And a king? They will demand you claim one for the ceremony. Even if you don't mean to keep one, or decide on another later," she continued.

Lilith's eyes moved to where Asrian leaned against the back wall, staring at Lilith with amusement in his emerald depths. She turned her head to the council member, who frowned.

"Cade will offer for your hand if you are queen, he

has shown interest, even with everything that happened. He has made it known he will accept you still."

"I will worry about that when we get there."

"As you wish, my queen."

Chapter Seventeen

Lilith listened as the ceremony droned on. It was insane how much shit went into a crowning. Once she'd been handed the staff, and knelt for her crown, the crowd knelt, including the Horde, who had witnessed the entire event without commenting. Only Ryder and Synthia hadn't knelt, but then they were High Fae royalty and above her.

"I give the Court their Queen, Lilith of the Houses of Night and Shadows. Queen of the Night Court and heir of the Shadow Court," the priestess said, smiling at her as she continued. "Who do you choose to claim as your King?"

"I have a King already," she whispered thickly. "I have Asrian, Prince of the Horde, born son of Alazander the Murderous King, and brother of ruling Horde King Ryder, King of the Beast. If he'll reign at my side," she finished, not bothering to lift her eyes in case he rejected her claim.

"Beast King?" Ryder whispered in a hushed tone.

"Beast mode sounds interesting," Synthia uttered beneath her breath.

"Does he reject it?" someone in the audience whispered, and Lilith's face flamed with embarrassment. "I think he rejected her."

"I don't accept one year and a day," he growled beside her. "I accept you and your people, but not the timeline."

"Choosing a king is forever; eternity until death steals you from this world," the priestess whispered as if she was trying to keep the confusion down from the audience.

"You want me forever?" he asked, his hand forcing her chin to lift, to meet his stare. "And my children?"

"They'll create monsters, this is insane!" someone from the audience screamed.

"I'd cease your tongue before I remind you why I am King of the Horde, creature," Ryder hissed, and the audience went silent.

"My children will be your children, protected by the Horde. I have the Horde King's word on it; anyone who challenges or questions any child we produce will be given the option to accept my child, or leave Faery and enter the fires that burn in the next realm. That is why I asked it. That was what I needed to know so that when I took my throne, you'd be at my side, Asrian. Do you accept me?" Her eyes begged him, unable to put into words what she needed to because of the eyes on them. Weaknesses were used against those who exposed them. She'd rip the throat out of anyone who tried to harm him, but he'd rip her heart out if he rejected her.

"I accept you, Lilith. I accept this court and the

people. I will provide for them where the last king failed, and I will give you strong sons to defend this court with. I have the strength of the Horde at my back, which will also defend this court in the way it has since the first tithe was made to my grandfather and the Horde. I accept you forever."

"This isn't a wedding," Sinjinn hissed from the crowd. "Fucking kiss her already and let's get these guys some food. They're starving and starting to look at us like we're the food."

"It is done then. I give you your King and Queen of the Night Court. The Horde and the Court of Night have prepared a feast fit for kings. Join us, toast to a new court, and a new rule."

Once the people had begun to rush towards the great hall for a seat, Lilith worried her bottom lip with her teeth as Asrian stared at her.

"You chose me," he said.

"I like you in my bed," she shrugged as a smile tugged at her lips.

"Is that so?"

She smiled and looked up at him. "I know you don't love me, and I'm not sure if what I feel is love or not yet. I also know the higher courts don't marry for love, only bloodlines and alliances. But I want you, and when you walked away from me in the bedroom, it left an ache I never want to feel again. I want to see where this goes; I want to know you and have a chance to make this work. If it doesn't work out, well, the Horde King is your brother, so you'll have an out. Isn't that what you called what you offered me? For the record, I can hear the whispers in every shadow of every court. I am the

Shadow Queen's heir."

"I don't know about love, but I know you're mine. I don't want anyone else. But this thing, I want this with you. I want to be in your bed too, even if I am your heathen king."

"I'd like you there, heathen king. I think we may need to borrow your brother's title tonight," she laughed as they started towards the hall where the feast was in full effect. Lilith paused on the stairs, looking to where her mother and sister served the starving members of the court as the higher lords watched them in horror.

It was surreal standing in the hallway where the Horde King had so long ago beaten her mother. Now, the new king stood beside his queen who spoke to the kids as she waved her hand and plates laden with food would appear before them. The laughter was contagious as she stared at her people.

"You will be amazing because if not, I'll be the first to tell you just how much you suck," Asrian said with a chuckle beside her as he slipped his hand into hers. "Sometimes bad things happen, and after enough time has passed, good things take their place and the bad is a little easier to deal with. You lost a parent tonight, but you gained one back. You gained someone who thinks you hung the moon and stars, with a little anger as you hung them, but for me, you hung them in that sky."

"Who taught you to talk like that?" she laughed as she turned and placed her hands into his.

"I watched Ryder grovel to get his queen, and when you want something as much as I want you, a little wooing is needed."

"This is going to be quite an adventure with you,

isn't it?"

"I promise to keep you on your toes, wife."

"And I promise to keep you happy and well-fed, my sweet heathen king."

"Promise?" he asked as he pulled her against his body.

"I promise."

~ The End ~

About the Author

Amelia lives in the great Pacific Northwest with her family. When not writing, she can be found on her author page, hanging out with fans, or dreaming up new twisting plots. She's an avid reader of everything paranormal romance.

Stalker links! Want to keep up on what I am doing? Follow me below and watch for author updates.

Facebook: https://www.facebook.com/authorameliahutchins
Website: http://amelia-hutchins.com/
Amazon: http://www.amazon.com/Amelia-Hutchins/e/B00D5OASEG
Goodreads: https://www.goodreads.com/author/show/7092218.Amelia_Hutchins
Twitter: https://twitter.com/ameliaauthor
Pinterest: http://www.pinterest.com/ameliahutchins
Instagram: https://www.instagram.com/author.amelia.hutchins/
Facebook Author Group: https://goo.gl/BqpCVK

Printed in Great Britain
by Amazon